Growing up in rural Nova Scotia, Darlene Hawes was rooted in the foundation of possibilities. She completed her graduate and post-graduate work in Halifax and used her skill sets as a school psychologist and certified child play therapist working with children and their families. As a registered counselor, she held a private practice for ten years before retiring. She is also a graduate of the Assisi Institute in Connecticut. Darlene enjoys cooking and entertaining but during the pandemic restraints she cooked up a book of short stories instead. Her happiest times are spent with her family and dear friends.

This book is dedicated to my late husband, Herbert D. Whitman, with my gratitude and love. Thanks for the stories, joys, tears, laughter, unwavering friendship, and devotion you gave to me and our family. Thank you for our wonderful sons; I still see you in them. I will always remember you and how you filled up my senses.

Darlene Hawes

MANIFESTING MEMORIES

A Collection of Short Stories

AUSTIN MACAULEY PUBLISHERS™
LONDON • CAMBRIDGE • NEW YORK • SHARJAH

Copyright © Darlene Hawes 2023

All rights reserved. No part of this publication may be reproduced, distributed, or transmitted in any form or by any means, including photocopying, recording, or other electronic or mechanical methods, without the prior written permission of the publisher, except in the case of brief quotations embodied in critical reviews and certain other non-commercial uses permitted by copyright law. For permission requests, write to the publisher.

Any person who commits any unauthorized act in relation to this publication may be liable to criminal prosecution and civil claims for damages.

This is a work of fiction. Names, characters, businesses, places, events, locales, and incidents are either the products of the author's imagination or used in a fictitious manner. Any resemblance to actual persons, living or dead, or actual events is purely coincidental.

Ordering Information
Quantity sales: Special discounts are available on quantity purchases by corporations, associations, and others. For details, contact the publisher at the address below.

Publisher's Cataloging-in-Publication data
Hawes, Darlene
Manifesting Memories

ISBN 9781649799517 (Paperback)
ISBN 9781649799531 (ePub e-book)
ISBN 9781649799524 (Audiobook)

Library of Congress Control Number: 2022916517

www.austinmacauley.com/us

First Published 2023
Austin Macauley Publishers LLC
40 Wall Street, 33rd Floor, Suite 3302
New York, NY 10005
USA

mail-usa@austinmacauley.com
+1 (646) 5125767

Heartfelt thanks to those who read all my stories and offered thoughtful criticism and helpful critiques that enriched the storytelling. Special thanks to David and Carmel Edison, Faye Hawes, and Donna Ward for their honesty and assistance with editing and organizing some of my thoughts. I am mindful and grateful to all those family and friends (you know who you are) who read some of the stories and delighted me with your valuable discussions. My deep gratitude to Aaron Whitman for his technical help and support. To Austin Macauley Publishers and all others who have helped make this book a reality, I am grateful to each one of you.

Table of Contents

Light Shines on Scars and Other Hidden Things	11
On Being a Widow	25
Psychic Fare	40
Witnessed	55
Let Us Remember	74
The Post Office	89
Just So You Know	103
Rewards	124
Keep Your Eyes Peeled	148

Light Shines on Scars
and Other Hidden Things

It was Saturday morning and her little five-year-old legs were running up the stairs obeying her mother's command to go wake up the boys. These three older brothers, who were sleeping in so late, were all in their early twenties, and were probably out late last night with their girlfriends. Nevertheless, morning was slipping away and breakfast was to be over with before afternoon arrived. She ran all the way to the back bedroom which belonged to the older boys. The five-bedroom house grew as the family of fourteen children grew. Like everything else, bedrooms needed to be shared. As she opened the bedroom door, she noticed the beam of sunlight shining through the opening in the not completely closed curtains. She leapt upon the bed perching herself atop the blankets over her brother who slept in the middle. He wasn't the youngest of the three but he slept in the middle as if protection surrounded him. As she pulled the blankets away from their faces, she yelled to them, in her outside voice, "Mama said you have to get up, right now!" Suddenly, for the first time, she saw his scars and gasped. Their eyes met. She whispered, "What happened?"

He sleepily answered, "I had operations when I was little because I had polio."

She understood "little". But "operations", "polio"? These words meant nothing to her. Her eyes glanced to the brothers on either side of him. Their eyes were opened, staring away, but listening.

She looked back at him. In her innocence and compassion, she asked, "Does it hurt?" He answered, "No." There was a silence. Something was left hanging in that brief "no," something that was unspoken and had to settle in and be understood when the time was ready. She would come to appreciate that the hurt was not in the scarring, but in the unfairness that had befallen him; in how he had to adapt, overcome and be strong in ways other boys didn't.

As soon as it was sufficient for a child's attention to be given to this concern, she re-addressed the purpose of her intrusion; "Well, you guys have to get up now because Mama said so!" She slid off the bed and ran out the door leaving it open behind her.

In her recollections, nothing more was ever said or thought about it. On the warm summer days when other boys took their tee shirts off to let the sun warm their bodies, his shirt remained on as both his warmth and protection.

Polio, caused by a virus that only affected people, made its first appearance in Canada in 1910. By the 1920s, it had traveled across the country from the West coast into every part of the country. Children under age ten were usually the ones affected by it. If it invaded the nervous system and spinal cord it could completely paralyze them. In 1955, Canadian scientists produced the first polio vaccine that was proven to prevent "the crippler," as it was known. By 1965 there were almost no cases of polio in this country. Canada was one of the first Countries to completely wipe out the disease.

It was a couple of years later when his little sister became aware that he walked with a limp and was "crippled." Something she had not noticed until now, as she did not make a connection to the earlier information she had learned. Therefore, she did not associate the way he walked with having had polio or the scars she had seen years ago. She simply realized now that she had grown taller and believed she could run pretty fast. She knew she could not run faster than her younger brother or the older one who was next to her in age. But they weren't crippled.

One day when a new calf was born all four of them were going to the barn to see it. The two youngest boys took off running toward the barn. In her childish audacity she turned to her brother, sixteen years her senior, and challenged him to a race to the barn. He laughed and said he didn't want to race to the barn. She took his refusal as cowering and convinced herself she really could beat him in a race. At six years old, she didn't know any better.

"Okay, then let's just race to the field and back," she insisted. The field was only across the yard. Again, he said no, and she kept it up. Belligerently, she told him that he didn't want to race her because he knew she'd beat him.

Finally, he accepted the challenge. He said, "Okay; but just to the field and back." They got ready.

She called out, "On your mark, get set, go!" She took off at what seemed like lightning speed to her. He never let her get too far ahead, but just enough that she needed to do a shoulder check once or twice to see how much of a lead she had. When they reached the grass of the field, the halfway mark, they were on a slight incline running back across the yard to the house. Just as she was approaching the well, maybe ten meters from the finish line, he made his move. He went flying by her like she was standing still. She likely would have stood still if it hadn't been for the momentum that kept her moving because she was in awe and disbelief of what she was seeing. She wanted to stop and stare as she saw him touch the back porch ahead of her. He was laughing so hard, seemingly about his win, that she felt delighted for him.

She called out, "You beat me! You're a really fast runner. I didn't know you could run so fast!" He continued laughing as he put his arms around her and gave her a hug. She was happy for him. Then, she skipped ahead of him as they walked to the barn.

It was sometime later when she was thinking about the race, the truth dawned on her. The truth of what a little brat she had been. Because he had a handicap, she made the ridiculous assumption that she would do better than him in a race. He didn't need to or want to prove what he was capable of, but he was clever enough to recognize a teachable moment. In the kindest and most loving way of fulfilling her request and challenge, he taught his little sister a lesson she needed to learn, through an experience she would never forget. Hold your judgement; you might be wrong. That's the sort of thing good, big brothers do. They teach the younger ones important things they need to know; like what real strength and power looks like.

Little sis had a scar of her own which she was oblivious to at the time. She was only about two years old when it occurred. Her baby brother had arrived to share their parents' bedroom. It was time for her to snuggle into the double bed with four of her older sisters ranging in age from nine to fourteen. It has been said that only pups and kittens who trust one another will cuddle up and sleep together. She would add sisters to that statement.

On a week-day night one of the girls brought a glass of water to the bedroom and left it sitting on the nightstand beside the bed. As little ones are prone to do, the two-year-old woke early and got out of bed to go climb in bed with her mother. In her sleepy stumbling, she knocked the glass of water off the stand and it broke as it hit the floor. She landed on top of the broken glass wedging a piece of it into her behind. Now everybody was awake. Fortunately, this memory did not stay with her, but the scar on her behind did. Had her daddy been home, he would have driven to the general store for the bandages and ointment needed for her care, for he had purchased his first vehicle the same year she was born. Instead, the fourteen-year-old sister had to run to the store and hurry back with the needed supplies to help mend the wound. This, too, was a scar that most people would never see. But everyone has scars they carry that they never let anyone see.

At the time she received her scar, her brother with the polio scars was about eighteen years old. The older boys in the family, like in most rural families, attended school until about grade ten. Not only did they need to get work and become more self-sufficient, the rural country teachers were usually not qualified to teach a grade higher than ten, in the one-room schools that housed all the students from kindergarten through grade ten. One of the older girls in the family left home and moved to the city with family friends so she could complete her high school. An uncle once said that when he was in grade ten, he asked his teacher a math question and she could not answer it. He concluded she didn't know any more than he did, so he quit school. He went on to be the general contractor for schools and hospitals that were later built in the area. After grade ten, the older boys in the family found work and boarding in the city and had to spend their week-days there.

The three youngest boys were at home, and the older boys still came home on the weekends. It was fun when they were around. There was more of an abundance of music, laughter and playfulness when they were there. It may have been part of their own delight of being at home with the rest of the family. It seemed the girls always had to work a lot both on week-days and week-ends. There was a colloquial saying that went "a woman's work is never done." It may have been that they did more than their share of the work.

One brother had bought a guitar and was teaching himself and a younger, interested brother how to play it: to learn some chords. In 1961, they could pick Johnny Cash's Tennessee Flat Top Box very well. The brother who had had polio also liked music. He seemed to prefer, at least for a time, the songs of Tennessee Ernie Ford. He would sing Sixteen Tons and Big Bad John when these tunes were hits in the mid to late fifties. There was a resemblance between him and Tennessee Ernie Ford. They seemed to look alike from pictures featured on record albums, with their black hair and steady eyes, but in her opinion, her brother was more handsome with his blue eyes and big smile. He also liked to sing the funny songs and seemed to get a kick out of playfully singing them to his younger siblings. He seemed to appreciate the humor in Jim Ed Brown's song, "Looking Back to See," when he sang it. He laughed at what must have been the honesty he could visualize in such an experience.

By the time she was ten years old, this brother who once sang funny songs to her, had fallen in love with a beautiful young woman who adored him as much as he did her. Within a year of their marriage, they were blessed with twins, a girl and a boy. Someone asked him which one was born first. He said it was his daughter because his son was a gentleman and let her go first. The joyful and loving spirit he carried seemed to make invisible any scars or handicap.

Not all the scars that occurred in the family were results of disease or accidents. Some scars were more hidden; what might be called the psychological kind – wounds that cut so deeply yet leave no physical evidence of themselves. Despite all those wounds, it may be safe to say that things often worked out, as circumstances provided, for the convenience and enrichment of all. At least that is the positive spin one must put on difficult situations. A spin that creates the appearance of strength, and the belief that maybe you can "fake it till you make it."

After the early death of their mother, there were four younger children, three boys and a girl, remaining at home. The oldest ones were married, working or gone off to college. Of the four still living at home, the oldest was by nature a free and adventurous young man of fifteen. He, too, like his older brothers before him, did his duties around home and for the family. In particular, he could be relied upon to milk the cows. At times, if his younger siblings bothered him while he sat on the stool doing his task, he might turn a teat toward them, spraying them with a little milk until they squealed and ran.

He had been outside, after supper, when he learned of his mother's death. The mother of a friend of his had obviously been listening in on the telephone party line when the Doctor called from the hospital, and received the news at the same time the family did. She told her son who ran outside and informed his friend, not that he should go home now, but that his mother was dead. The shock, disbelief and overwhelming devastation he felt, had numbed him as he ran for home. He was angry and heart-broken. His free spirit became a wild and broken spirit. With no mother in the home to love, discipline and understand this boy the way she did, he was adrift. While it was an event that put all of their lives in upheaval, for him, nothing seemed to matter anymore. He no longer wanted to go to school, nor did he care what time, or even if, the cows were milked. The dad decided that it was necessary for this brother to be under his wing as there was no one else who could adequately watch over him. He was taken out of school and went to work in the woods at a lumber camp with his dad. The wounds on the inside aren't exposed to the air and seem to take a longer time to heal, if they ever do.

With this teenage brother now gone, there was no one at home anymore who was old enough and able to care for the cows, horse or pigs. The hens were kept for another year or so, and still provided eggs and the occasional chicken dinner. The two youngest brothers and their sister could still tend to the hens. It was another sad day when she overheard her dad in a discussion with some older siblings about the price of scratch feed. The cost had risen so much that it no longer made sense to keep the hens. On that day she came to a full and painful awareness that the life she had known was over. They were the only family in the community who had not moved forward with the post war boom. They had maintained and still cared for the animals that cared for them, and continued to grow their own vegetables. But with King, the horse gone, there was no assistant to help plow the field. Some might think that the animals didn't care for them, and that this anthropomorphic suggestion is distasteful. Yet, anyone having a close, interactive relationship with any living thing on a daily basis could not avoid the perspective of a mutual caring. Other families in the community had come to rely on their independent grocer. It would be hard for her to conceive of the notion that the independent grocer cared for them more than the animals did. The animals were not concerned about cash flow. What flowed was what they gave to each other. With the animals gone, they had now joined the ranks of what she considered "the poor." Although some would have described them as a family who "didn't have a pot to piss in," she would wonder what they knew about self-sufficiency. They were sustainable long before it ever became cool. It was the early sixties, and the first time she had ever felt that life was hard.

Life with her big brother, sister-in-law and their beautiful babies made the transition to a new way of life easier. Because they came to live in the family home, until their own home was ready, the youngest children could remain living in the only home they ever knew. The roles seemed to have been reversed, and now they were the older kids doing their part to help out with the younger ones, not their siblings, but their niece and nephew. Being able to help feed the babies, rock them and sing to them brought back the enfoldment of love that once surrounded them. To be cared for and nurtured was what they had known and the circle was re-established in a new time and in a new way.

Their sister-in-law was a wonderful person and an inspiration. She was only about twenty-three years old yet she managed to care competently and lovingly for her two babies and three pre-adolescent children. She ran the household efficiently and effectively. Their older brother, her husband, traveled into the city five days a week through storms, fog and all kinds of weather to provide for his wife and children. He always walked with a limp, but there was nothing "crippled" about that man!

For many years he continued to drive in and out of the city for work. On his daily drive, he usually had a carload of passengers also traveling to the city to work. All those men wanted to be home with their wives and children at the end of each day. They didn't carpool, exactly, because it was always her brother and his car; but they did travel together. There were no seatbelts in the vehicles in those days, but the car was roomy and carried six adults comfortably. He usually had four or five passengers each day. He and his family had moved into their own home by this time. On several occasions when she was old enough to go into the city on her own, she would ask him if he had any room to take her and if she could get a drive back home with him the same evening. He always checked with his passengers to see if one of them might happen to be taking their own vehicle to the city on the day in question. It seems she was always very lucky, as he never had to refuse her. There was always room on the days she wanted a drive with him. Only once was it crowded; and she had been given the option. One of the passengers was only traveling halfway to the city, so it seemed justified and agreeable to everyone that she should go as they would only be crowded for half the way. It worked out fine. He would drop her off and pick her up at a conveniently arranged spot. Always reliable.

There were a couple of occasions, when some troublesome phone calls came for her sister-in-law. Her teenage brother and her dad were in conflict. One or both were drinking excessively. Either her mother or her sister was calling asking for her husband to intervene. Each time, she hung up the phone and asked him if he would go help. He didn't want to, but felt he must do what he could. He, probably also, wanted to honor the trust and confidence she had in him. He was a kind, reasonable and level-headed man. He was the one, most likely, to calm turbulent waters.

Throughout his life he continued to do all the activities his polio-free brothers and friends did like fishing and hunting and participation in sports. He didn't keep up with the others, he out-hunted and out-fished them most of the time. He was an avid sportsman. He did not play softball like the other boys. Instead, he was the umpire of their games. He had a good eye, good judgement and a fair perspective. He was trusted and respected. He became an Official Umpire of the Nova Scotia Softball Association. He set a good example for all.

It was many years later when, for the first and only time, she heard their father speak about how he and their mother prayed for their little boy's recovery from polio. He was their fifth child, the sixth one was a toddler at home and the seventh was growing safely inside their mother's womb. At that time, the oldest of their children was ten. The transportation for this young family was live horse-power. They owned no motorized vehicle. Their little boy had been in the hospital many months having surgeries and recovering from them. His stay included a Christmas. They had no way or means to visit with him in the city hospital. No one had ever heard that anyone offered to drive them to the hospital or to stay with and care for their other children at home while they went to see their son. The gratitude they would have felt for such a generous offer would have been spoken of and made known to the family throughout the years. It just didn't happen. It may be that no one else had the time or the means to be so gracious. It was wartime and there was a lot of rationing. But most likely it was because the disease was contagious. When someone in a family got polio, the family had to post a sign on the door telling people to stay away. Whether a sign was posted or not, word would get around in a small community, and no one would come near. It was later in life when an older sibling remarked, with heartfelt sadness, that she couldn't understand how her parents could leave their little boy in the hospital over Christmas and not even go visit him. It is the kind of thing people express when their own love and emotions overwhelm their reasoning; when another place and time is superimposed on the circumstances and context of a previous, incomprehensible situation. It's that futile imagining of how the past might have been different. The past can never be changed. But to live and choose well in the present is a way to mold a better future. Tend to your scars and get on with living. In their circumstances and in their moment in time, the parents gave all they had. They prayed, while they "carried water and chopped wood." This Buddhist expression may have been literal for them.

At the time of their father's death, when this brother and his youngest sister embraced each other, she cried. With wet eyes and mustering the strength to speak, he said to her, "Don't cry. You know Dad would want us to be strong."

It was only ten years later when she would say goodbye to this brother. He was only seventy-three. A ninety-year-old woman, well known to the family, approached her at his wake. She said what a darling little boy he had been. She explained that she had been a Registered Nurse working at the hospital when he was being treated for polio. On her last shift, before she left to get married and move to another Province, she went to see her favorite little patient. She said she asked him if there was anything he needed or anything she could get for him. He told her, "A flashlight."

She added, "He was afraid of the dark." She continued to explain that she couldn't get him one because she was leaving that night and wouldn't be back, but she let someone know so they would tell his parents. She then asked the sister, "Do you know if he ever got a flashlight?"

Sister answered, "I don't know." What she didn't say was that she wouldn't be born for another twelve years or so and that nobody ever told her about the flashlight. She would like to think he got a flashlight. But not knowing, she chooses to believe that the particular darkness he experienced was overcome by the light of love that surrounded him then and for the rest of his life. It was not always a light he could see but one that he was aware of and felt in his heart. It was more than a flash. It was a light that never burned out for him. Like the beam of sunlight through parted curtains, the light found its way inside.

Not long ago, the little sister was walking through an airport pulling her luggage beside her. Coming toward her was a handsome looking man pulling his luggage beside him. They kept flashing glances toward each other. She thought he was a sight to behold. As they passed by each other they shared a smile. She could not resist the urge to turn around and have one last look at him. As she did so, he was turned around having one last look at her. They both burst out laughing. In that gifted moment, she experienced a flash of memory transporting her back to the late 1950s as she could see and hear her brother laughing as he sang, *I Was Looking Back to See.* (Jim Ed Brown, 1958).

His light still shines, and a never-ending love lights up her life and keeps her strong.

On Being a Widow

"Have you ever thought that you might remarry?" This is a question I have heard from several friends and some family members. Every time I am asked this, or think of it, it stirs a whirlpool of emotions, and triggers fears of leaving behind all I have left of him. I know their intent. They don't want to see me sad. They want me to project my thoughts and myself into a future of possibilities. Some of them even have a lonely old male friend they'd like to hook me up with. Entertaining their queries all seems to be a part of "closing out a life." Now, that's an expression! I believe it is intended to reference closing out the affairs of the deceased. But it feels like a punch in the gut to hear it. I'm not just closing out his life. It means that I, too, have to close out a part of my life. Embedded in this phrase, and stinging the rawness in me, is the need to try to build a new life, without him.

When you become a widow, you must face people and situations you don't want to face. You must steel yourself and be tempered so you are strong enough to endure the looks and words others carelessly send your way. At first it catches you off-guard; then you learn to read the thoughts and pity in the eyes of friends and neighbors while you try to maintain your composure and act like you can handle it all. It helps others believe you are strong, and will be okay. They need to know that. It is reassuring for them to know that you still carry all the good attributes they've assigned to you. You find yourself taking on that responsibility to ensure there is no dissonance in their concept of you. I don't know why that is. Maybe you, unconsciously, fear losing them too. If others see how distraught you really are, they may not be able to endure it. Some people look at you from a distance, as if you were a leper and they don't want to catch what has befallen you. As if losing a spouse might be contagious. Maybe they're just lost for words. They've never seen you at your weakest; never seen you crumble; and they never will. The only one who ever witnessed that naked vulnerability in you is gone now. When you collapse into the depths of grief, more helpless than a child, there are no mother's arms or lover's arms to hold you tightly and safely. It feels like the pull of quicksand taking you under. You know you better have something strong and solid to get a grip on because you've got to pull yourself out of it.

It seems to me that there was some depth of understanding of this grief in the choice of music played by the ship's band while the Titanic sank. They played The Widow's Waltz.

Tonight, in this dimly lit room, after a good portion of this bottle of Apothic Dark, I get lost in my reflections. To create the illusion of not being alone, I consider all those who, like myself, are only totally honest with themselves when their inhibitions are slumbering and their egos are too weakened to put up a defense. The clear, unadulterated truth we all need to face, and can't help but face in these moments. This is the time when the soul's clarity comes through, for the soul is never intoxicated and is always truthful. This is what we truly seek to console us when all the bullshit is sedated. This is where we really sit in our pain and our honest awareness of how we try to camouflage it. This is also where we face our lack of courage. This space that holds our truth because it is the place where the witness resides. For me, my witness remains aloof to the world where I laugh and dance and pretend I'm okay, and to the world where I am all alone, and ghosts haunt me. It just observes and notices it all. In either world I can convince myself that it feels better, momentarily, to be inebriated to disguise the truth that lonesomeness prevails. But this behavior does not go unnoticed either. I cannot escape the constant reminder that my life has fallen short of the fullness of its dreams. There is no growing old together, no more quiet moments alone having tea and a snack, no more drying his back when he, surprisingly, realizes how good the rubbing feels and then needs a complete back massage, no watching our grandchildren grow and sharing in their milestones with them. There are so many dreams that have died with him.

I have to recalibrate.

Earlier today, I intended to go to the garden center to get soil and a large pot for an avocado plant. About three months ago I cut into an avocado and discovered a seed that was already sprouting. In my excitement, I took it out to the patio and dug a spot in the soil next to the chives. There it is; about thirty centimeters tall now. The goddamn thing is determined to grow! Doesn't it know this isn't Mexico or California. It doesn't seem to care how far north it is. My heart and soul feel so much compassion for it. I don't want it to die in the cold frost that will arrive in only a few weeks. My computer, my dearest late-night friend, told me an avocado will grow as much as sixty-six feet tall, and it will take six years to bear fruit. I felt defeated. Then I discovered that an avocado can be a houseplant. How limited is that? It's like turning it into a eunuch. I have allowed this to grow, but it can never reach its potential. I have created something that can be enjoyed for my own pleasure, but it can never realize its own dream. No wonder I opened that wine tonight. I must have needed something to dull the ouch of this mirroring. From now on, every avocado seed is going into the compost before it gets any ideas of sprouting here in the north.

Perhaps a shift in attitude will help me. I may need to drop the resistance and accept that life requires strength and courage because it makes us no promises of joy and fulfillment. Life is going to lambaste every living thing with disappointment, failure and loss. I need to ask myself, "Do you think you are strong enough to handle life?" If you're not, you won't be here long, or you'll be miserable while you're here. Isn't endless change the inherent nature of existence? This, too, shall pass. Before I arrived here, in this world and this life, I was non-existent; and the day I die, I will be non-existent again. As Mark Twain implied, death shouldn't bother us because it didn't bother him before he got here. Maybe that's the rub. It may be that we love our existence and never want to leave it, regardless of the misery it brings us. But leave it, we must. And while we remain here in this existence, we will be flooded with grief. When will that change? When the next round of grief comes? How can we get through it? Sometimes, it seems to just come out of nowhere.

I've tried to honor it and give grief its time; allow it to overtake me if it needs to. It never seems to tire itself out. It just tires me out. I can't seem to get control of it some days. Many widows, from good and long marriages, have told me that you never get over it; you just learn to live with it. The only widow I know, who has remarried, said something similar to me, but added that she is happy with her new husband. His presence in her life fills up the emptiness. Some part of me understood her words. I felt I knew that place of emptiness she spoke of. But to the unfamiliar she may have received a response like, "you should have got yourself a pet." Those who did not know the emptiness she had come to know would not understand.

I am told that what's meant to be will be. If some guy comes into my life, I will know if he is meant for me. The only guys around here are Ben and Jerry chilling their sweetness in my freezer. I know they're meant for me! When I open the door, there they are wearing that jacket that says "Cherry Garcia." Easy boys! Tonight the temptation feels overwhelming. Maybe it's the wine. But I may surrender to their deliciousness soon.

It wasn't too late when I went to bed. I slept soundly. I don't even feel like I have a wine hangover. But it's another one of those mornings where I can't gather the energy to face the world pretending it's alright, or pretending that he's still here. Telling myself, until I feel convinced, that I know life goes on, and I will too. Today, like so many days, I don't care if I do go on. Some days I've been able to tell myself the most positive and encouraging things, I am almost believable. It enables me to face the day in my fantasy of the moment. On those days I can joke and laugh, talk to friends and family on the phone and even prepare nutritious meals for myself. I can dress up and look very presentable, even attractive. People greet me with delight and tell me how wonderful I look. Some even have the presumptuousness to say, "You're doing great!" They have no idea the effort and tenacity it takes to present so favorably to the world and keep the pain hidden. Either I am a great pretender or I've missed my calling in Hollywood.

Each day ends usually with mixed emotions of great relief and deep sorrow. The relief comes from a flicker of hope that as time passes and another day is over, it will bring me closer to the hurt easing. Time heals all things. Another great saying, if you can force yourself to believe it. Sometimes it is tomorrow when I turn the light out, and my sobbing begins.

I keep the radio on for company, and I do enjoy the music. From morning until night my favorite radio station has programming that carries all genres of music, and music through the decades. Yesterday morning, George Jones was belting out, *A Picture of Me Without You.* As I listened, I thought, A damn apt description George! I have not only watched it. I have been that child with the broken heart. That was an abyss that my siblings and I were thrown into when our mother died. There are always the comforters. They are wonderful. But no one can fill that place. There remains an emptiness, like a black hole within you.

I wonder if anyone who has not experienced this kind of loss can know or understand what it does to you. How could they? Hell, I've experienced it, and I don't understand it. People try hard to be understanding and compassionate, but the emptiness that's created from losing such a deep, connected and soulful love remains insatiable. Sometimes it feels tiresome just trying to sort and make sense of the caring comments. Things like "It must be hard," and "This sorrow is to be expected." Seriously? How does anyone expect the sorrow that comes from falling into an abyss? You can't even expect the abyss.

Suddenly gone: the presence of someone you trust completely; the whisper of a thought or a plan for tomorrow; a gentle hand brushing hair away from your face to kiss you goodnight; someone who would fart and try to blame it on you, and would swear there must be someone under the bed rather than admit to his own offensive odors; someone who would nuzzle up to you for warmth; and when you open your eyes in the morning you'd see his adoring face smiling at you and saying, "Good morning." And it was a good morning when you could get up and live your life authentically.

It has been well over a year since I have been living alone. I sit outside and listen to the birds singing and feel the morning air before the breezes stir. As I look at nature all around me, it feels like nothing knows he's gone. The birds and trees and grass aren't waiting for him to come outside with his coffee and sit beside me. They just keep on doing what birds and trees and grass do. I think maybe I should try to take a lesson from them. Although I do keep trying to follow my daily routine, there is a need to be mindful of the unexpected; that your next step is not into a sinkhole. Like when you talk to your son about something and you casually say, "Well your father will know." A place where you could go that was once solid ground and where you walked with confidence. Now there is the fear of the unexpected emotional flood hitting you in the face.

Memories feel like they are both a blessing and a curse. One needs to be careful to keep hold of what is reality. It is easy to think of the many beautiful and happy moments, but I know I must not forget the hellish times too. Those moments of hurt, anger, pain, suffering and hatred; moments you never wanted to relive, but now you must make yourself remember to keep the balance and reality of what was your life. All of it formed the mosaic of our life together. In fact, it was in those difficult times when our love and commitment was tested. Those were the times that determined the depth of our feelings for each other. We learned we could endure anything together. Nothing was stronger than our love for each other.

Then death came along. As if! Does that dark fool think he could stop us? Oh, he changed things alright. But what death doesn't seem to know is that love is eternal. Just as death cannot be undone, neither can our love for each other. That bell can't be unrung! Every thought and so many occasions bring back memories of his sayings, like: "Well, we can't put the shit back in the horse." He was usually accurate whether inappropriate or not. It's true. What's done is done. However, we may find a use for it in the garden of our lives to help things grow.

Sometimes when he'd be in the garage immersed in a woodworking project, I knew he couldn't hear me call him to lunch so I'd walk out to tell him it was ready. As soon as he saw me, he'd put down whatever he was in the midst of doing, come toward me in his underwear shirt, overalls and cut off rubber boots and hug me, like he hadn't seen me in ages. But we had breakfast together. If there was a slow song playing on his music machine he had turned on, he'd take me in his arms and dance with me until it was over. We were in our mid-fifties, but he made me feel like I was twenty.

Anything can trigger the memories. Most of them reflect a mixture of his moods. He was a worrier. He was seriously funny, too. He had the foresight to see potential outcomes in any event. Sometimes it would be a funny imagining, but most often dread. Traveling with him was always a mixed bag of delight and frustration. The most consistent and reliably frustrating were those trips of returning home from another country and coming through Customs. While vacationing outside Canada, every time, I got the foreboding warning about how we couldn't exceed our limit, no matter how small the purchase was. If I said, "I spent seventy dollars; we have an eight-hundred-dollar limit each.

"Oh yeah," he'd say, "but it won't take long to reach the limit." This panic escalated on the day before departure. It was the day of packing and accounting. All sales slips had to be tallied and ready to be presented to the Customs officer. There was never any doubt, in his mind, that we would be called upon to account for every cent we spent on goods before we would be allowed back across the border. Breaking or skirting the rules and regulations made him feel uncomfortable, and he didn't like to venture there.

I recall we had pulled off the highway for fuel just before we reached the border crossing. We always filled up there whether we needed fuel or not. In fact, it was always the moment of the final accounting check. Were the receipts still in order or had they somehow gone askew since we got in our vehicle. The tension and anxiety in the cab of our Suburban was thick. I told him, he better lighten up or he was just going to draw attention to himself. I knew on this particular trip we were very close to our limits. He knew it too. For him, it's too close for comfort. I ask him, sarcastically, what he thinks they'll do to us if we are over; throw us in prison for the rest of our lives? I tell him, if we owe something, we'll just pay it. We got in line and waited until we were directed to pull forward to the next available Customs officer. The man was pleasant but official. We presented our passports to him; told him we had been vacationing and how long we had been there. Did we have any cigarettes or alcohol? No. Had we purchased anything we were bringing back into the country? Yes, a set of dishes, some tee-shirts and souvenirs. Okay. Welcome home! We were on our way.

As we drove away, I am thankful it was a male officer on duty as he, obviously, had no idea of the price of dishes at the Royal Doulton store, although, I reminded myself, they were on sale. Suddenly, I realize how silent we are. My husband hasn't even breathed a sigh of relief. Through the windshield, I see the sign: Welcome to Canada. We drive past it, and he breaks into song… I burst into laughter, and so did he. We were unable to speak for the next few kilometers as we were both laughing so hard. I did try to say to him, "I didn't even know that you knew The Rock Island Line, but you do sound like Johnny Cash." But I couldn't get the words out through my hoots of laughter. He asked me later what I was trying to say in the truck. By then, I was able to get it out. Then we had another good laugh. He still makes me laugh today, but only in my memories.

He enjoyed food and dining out which we often did. It was his favorite outing. He was always personable with the servers. He sometimes acted like the restaurant was his as he would tell them, in a kind way, how things could be improved. They always expressed appreciation or agreement. He became friendly with the servers and they liked to please him and call him by name. He made them laugh. Parmesan cheese was a favorite add on; he'd put it on most everything. Once when a young woman server was grating cheese on his pasta, she looked at him and said, "Say when." He didn't say "when."

After a lot of grating, she looked at him. He noticed and said, "When it looks like it's too much, double it." He offered to save her wrist by grinding it himself. She passed the grinder to him.

There is so much to miss; so much to remember; and so much to be grateful for.

He loved telling funny stories. He also loved hearing them because he enjoyed sharing them with others. He had a knack for noticing nuances and seeking sensory information from every experience. His talent was a treasure. He could share his experiences with you in such detail that you felt like you were there too. I miss listening to him tell the same story repeatedly. I never thought I'd say that. He was a storyteller, and he knew when he had his listener in his grip. Sometimes the listener's intensity would excite and encourage him. Then he would exaggerate the details and extrapolate from other stories, so much so, that even I would sit up and take notice of the changes to the tale. He never failed to get a laugh from his listeners, although I sometimes found myself walking out of the room and shaking my head. His aim was to entertain and please; and he did.

Memories will never allow a life to be "closed out." But I realize I must learn to contain the memories while I control their emergence. Perhaps the grieving is also to help develop this balancing act. And it is an act because I must act strong and somehow neutralize all those emotions that were real and shared between us. The years bring their own changes to our lives, but illness, with its pain and suffering, also brings mood and personality changes as well as physical ones.

The last three years he suffered from kidney failure. Regardless of the positive spin people put on dialysis, a life extender, the truth is, it's an end game. How long before the end probably depends on the medical profile. His was grim: Congestive heart failure with uncontrollable arrhythmia and two daily injections of insulin for diabetes which he did not manage well. Any cautions or suggestions coming from me could trigger anger or deep disappointment in him. There were times he just wanted to have some of the things he used to enjoy in life, like French fries. Too much deprivation along with physical misery made living for him seem questionable. My attempts to maintain "normalcy" in what was no longer a "normal" life or routine seemed to make him wonder if I understood how ill he was. Wanting to prepare me, he would sometimes say, "You know I'm not going to be around much longer." It was the thing I most disliked hearing. He knew how bad he felt. I saw how bad he felt for I had known this man a very long time.

I would tell him, "We don't know how long we have, but I do know we have today, and I want today to be the best it can be for us."

We had acquired a new habit of occasionally going to McDonald's for their delicious Earl Grey tea and then driving to the docks to watch the goings-on while we drank our tea. Our last anniversary together fell on a dialysis day. We had been married at three o'clock, and it was precisely that time I walked toward his bed in the dialysis unit with Earl Grey tea and an anniversary cake I made for us. He was so surprised and happy to see me. He said he was just about to call me. Every year for the past forty-six years, if we were not together at the time, he would call, at three o'clock on our special day, to wish me a happy anniversary. On this forty-sixth anniversary, he was thrilled to share our cake with the staff in the dialysis unit, and have me there by his side.

The steady decline in his health, over a number of years, resulted in various changes in our relationship, particularly in our intimate relationship. One night after brushing my teeth and readying for bed, I walked into the bedroom to find him sitting in the chair. With a very somber look on his face, he addressed me. He firmly stated, "I want you to go out and get a man you can have sex with." Fortunately, I had made it to the bed and had something to support me as I looked at him in disbelief. He continued with, "You really shouldn't have to do without because of me."

I stared at him and uttered, "Is that what you would want if I was the one who had health issues?"

He came toward me protesting, "Oh, no, no. Never!"

As we stood close to each other, I looked him in the eyes and said, "For better or worse. That was the deal. That's how it still is with me." A look came over his face; a mixture of feelings congealed together; sadness, shame and relief. He wrapped his arms around me and held me close. As we released our hold, our eyes met, and I said, "There are lots of ways we can show our love for each other." We kissed. That subject was closed out.

As thoughts pass through my mind about moving forward in life with a new partner, whether it is to be or not, I have that memory that tells me he would not mind. In life and death all he has ever wanted was my happiness. Remembering him is part of my happiness. I realize I have to and can only live in the Now, so I have to let him go. But I will never let his memory go. How could I? He is entwined with my life, and I'm still here. Remembering him allows me to hold on to a life I have lived. A life lived with him that was full and satisfying.

The oldies station on the radio is playing Andy Williams singing, *How Sweet the Memories You Gave to Me.* It may be true that everything happens when it's meant to.

All through our marriage, for no reason I could ever figure out, he would say to me, "Nobody could ever love you as much as I do." Sometimes I would just laugh at him, and he would get very serious and say, "I mean it! There is no one, and there will never be anyone who could love you as much as I do." Baffled by his emphatic certainty, which seemed to have no context, I decided he must feel overwhelmed by the love he has for me. One day I decided to challenge his assertion.

When he said, "No one could love you like I do," I said, "How do you know that? There is no way you can know that with such certainty. You'd have to be able to measure that in some way and you can't." He said it didn't matter because no matter how much anyone could imagine or think they loved me; he would still love me more. To him, it was just impossible to fathom that anyone could ever feel more love than the love he felt for me.

This remained true even on the day we went for a drive because his spirits were low, and he needed to get out. During the drive he made a couple of negative remarks. I clarified with what I knew to be more reasonable or correct information. Then he said, "I hope I live long enough to be right about something with you." Surprised, I quickly considered how often I correct him, or if this was an exaggeration: a trait he was prone to. Regardless, he was feeling hurt. Perhaps he was just wanting to vent and say some outrageous things because of the mood he was in. Sometimes he did that. Usually, I understood when this happened and would just let it be. I made a mental note to not comment unless I could make an honest agreement with him. He soon gave me the opportunity, and I had the chance to say, "Yeah, I think you're right." He was quick, but I saw it register with him. We both adjusted our frustration levels and spoke more kindly. It's what love does; and we knew love.

Psychic Fare

Hey Doreen, *The Psychic Fair's next weekend. Wanna go?* Donna and I had gone to the Psychic Fair for the past two years and always had fun. She knew I would want to go; it was just a matter of which day of the weekend would work best. I answered her text with *Let's go Saturday.* Wanting to learn more about it, I went online to see who would be there with their holistic treatments and psychic insights. I found a recent article from a local paper about the organizer of the Fair. She, herself, was a medium who channeled messages from the other side, and she would be giving a talk at the event. I thought it might be nice to connect with some of my loved ones who have passed on, and decided, immediately, I would be there at ten o'clock, when the doors opened, so I'd be sure to book an appointment time with her before her schedule was filled.

    The week passed quickly. It is now Saturday morning and ten minutes before ten as I turn into the parking lot where the fair is being held. My phone rings. I press the picture of a telephone receiver on my steering wheel. Funny how this icon represents an older style phone and doesn't look like a cell phone at all. Upright, it means "answer;" horizontally, it means, "hang up" or "disconnect." Even young people who have never seen or used this type of phone know how to handle this iconic or "archaic" information. Some images seem to provide more intuitive clarity than others. It's Donna. She tells me she is running late and won't be there for ten o'clock. We'll meet up inside the venue, somewhere, when she arrives.

I stand in the line-up of about thirty people as the doors open. Waiting there in line holds that same anticipation of being fed a juicy piece of news shared by a friend who must swear you to secrecy before they will tell you. It brings that piquing curiosity that soon collapses into something you can do nothing with but hold the burden of knowing it. What's doubly troublesome is when you are told the same secret a few days later by another friend who follows the prerequisite of swearing you to secrecy before they will share the story with you. While you silently compare the information for confirmation, you feign interest and surprise. The line moves quickly, and soon I am inside paying my entrance fee and receiving my inked stamp on my hand. Moving out of the traffic area I survey the setting.

There is a curious excitement held in the mystery of the fragrant incense, homemade soaps, the flashing of fairy balls and glittering gemstones fashioned into earrings and bracelets. The sounding of Tibetan bowls, books, jewelry, oracle and tarot cards all in place at the various stations amidst Reiki treatments, Chakra alignments, Energy healers, essential oils and Watkins products. As I make my way through the rapidly filling room, the anticipation and seeking on the faces of other attendees, mostly women, mirror my own feelings. Unable to locate the medium I am searching for, I ask a couple of vendors if they know where she is. Both tell me she isn't doing readings this weekend, only the Public Talks. I am directed to where I may find her.

It is the first booth inside the entrance door and to my right. The medium I seek is not there. Her associates confirm the disappointing news I'd already been given. One of the women, the older of the two, arranging an exquisite jewelry display, stated, "I do readings, but I don't charge for them. If you want to buy a piece of jewelry, I'll give you a free reading." I know my reaction must look startling to her as I am thinking, *What? Doesn't she take this seriously?* I feel skeptical as I don't understand why she would give me a free reading. I just smile and examine the silver gargoyles and jewelry before I move on to a selection of scarves hanging above a nearby booth.

Now I am ready to leave, but still awaiting Donna's arrival. I decide to scan the signage on the reader's tables to see if there are other mediums in the group. All around me, women are signing up and filling the various schedules for readings. Suddenly, there it is. The sign: "Medium." I move, shoulder to shoulder, toward her sign-up sheet. No one has signed up here. Maybe I am just the first in her line; yet, I feel myself ignoring my better judgement. I ask about her offerings. I'm told that reaching those on the other side is primarily what she does. I sit down and pay the required fee.

She asks my first name and if there is someone I want to hear from. I tell her. She reflects a moment before she says, "He traveled a lot." She looks at me as if awaiting a response. I remain silent. Then she asks, "Didn't he travel a lot? Great distances?"

I reply, "He traveled for work and took a few vacation trips."

She then says, "He was a ship's captain."

I can't hold back my grin. I say, "You got the wrong guy!" Then, recalling what a joker my husband could be, I added, "Or he's pulling your leg."

She looks embarrassed and shaken. Then she asks, "Was there someone in your family who was a captain of a ship?"

I reply, "Not to my knowledge." She turns her head and stares away for a long moment. I'm thinking, *The only captain I know is Captain Morgan, and although spirited, he's safely locked up in my liquor cabinet at home.* Then she says her guide is giving me messages from my husband and that he wants me to live my best and fullest life. She continues but I interrupt her asking, "Don't you connect with those on the other side? Why are your guides telling you this?"

She answers, "They are passing on this information from him..." I really don't attend to what she is saying as my mind is thinking, *You took my forty-five dollars and this is the drivel I'm getting from you?*

I hear her say, "Do you have any questions you'd like to ask him?"

I stare at her while thinking, *He and I already have better communication than I'm getting here,* but I hear myself say, "No, I'm good. Thank you." I walk away. Think I better go look for Donna. I am glad to have a focus, and to hold in my mind that I am looking for Donna, otherwise I don't know where I may drift. I was left feeling dazed and dumb from this recent sketchy and unfulfilling experience. As I turn the corner to continue walking along the route laid out for the vendors, I spot Donna coming through the door.

She paid her entrance fee and is being stamped as I approach her.

The palm reader Donna wants to see is not at this event due to health issues. I had learned this during my earlier scouting through the layout of readers. Donna is disappointed, but we decide to do another walk around to find readers we may want to try. As we turn, Donna sees the jewelry display on our right. A beautiful bracelet catches her eye. While she's looking, I notice some pretty necklaces I had not seen earlier. The older woman looks at me and asks, "Are you the one who wanted a reading with me?"

I said, "Yes, I was here earlier."

She repeats. "If you buy a piece of jewelry, I'll give you a free reading, but it will have to be in a couple of hours." She notices that I have picked up and am holding one of the necklaces. Smiling, she comments; "I see you have *The Love Letter*." She proceeds to explain how all the jewelry was unique. The designs and motifs of each piece are from the period of 1840–1940. The watch faces and their inner workings are actual parts of old watches from that period. She says, "*The Love Letter* has the bird, symbolizing a lovebird, a messenger, and the key represents the key of the old-time mailboxes that were always locked with a key." Another young woman steps up to help us. I ask what the stones are. The one in my hand is a blue opal. There is another piece that has a pink opal, and the third necklace held a stone which had been formed from a volcanic eruption.

She did not name it. Donna, nodding to the piece in my hand, said, "You should get that one."

I answer, "I like it, but I almost never wear blue."

She then picks up the pink one and holds it against my neck. We both shake our heads. Then I pick up *The Love Letter* necklace with the volcanic stone, and we both say, "Wow." It seems to glow with the colors of hot burning embers: the red, gold, blue and the intermittent rainbow flickers with the bird flying atop it is captivating. I say, "I think I'll get this one and then I'll get my reading." Donna's birthday is approaching. She'll be twenty-nine again in just a couple of weeks. I tell her I want to get the bracelet she likes as a birthday gift for her. She won't hear of it as she feels it is too expensive a gift. I say, "I'm doing it, and then I'll know I gave you something you really like."

I ask the girl to process the sale. Donna protests, "But I have to buy something so I can get a free reading!" She picks up the necklace we had both admired and said, "Okay, I'm getting this for you!" We laugh. We both buy jewelry and then exchange the pieces with each other.

I say, "Happy Birthday. Put it on!"

Donna says, "I hope I'm still going to see you on my birthday."

I answer, "Of course. But don't waste a day of your life not enjoying the things you love!" We giggle as she puts the bracelet on her wrist. One of the things I enjoy immensely in life is the whimsy of women, and how we can laugh at our nonsensical behaviors.

We make our way around the crowded room and both sign up for the same psychic whose schedule is nearly full. It seems like a promising sign that she is in demand. We decide to go for tea and to return in time for our free reading with Maria.

When we return about an hour later, it seems as though Maria is already waiting for us. She is chatting with a couple of ladies but tells them she has an appointment with me. She motions me to a chair and says, "Have a seat." She looks at me, smiles and says, "I knew you were going to buy 'The Love Letter' the very first moment you walked up to the booth." Then she says, "You have three guides around you. Two are older women and one is a younger male. What is your ancestry?"

I answer, "I'm not Mediterranean as many people seem to think!"

"No, no. I don't think that. This older woman guide is an ancestor of yours, but she seems Norse." She looks perplexed. Then she says, "The young boy; do you know who he is?"

I say, "No."

She adds, "There is also a child; a very joyful, playful energy that's around you or seems to be a part of you. Did you ever have a miscarriage?"

I say, "No."

She then suggests that maybe the energy is just a part of my essence. She continues saying, "You have a very high vibration. Your aura is like an Indigo. You are traveling on your right path in life, and the path I see you on is very sparkly and golden. It's leading you to where you are supposed to go; to your goal: What you're supposed to be doing in life." I smile at her, silently wondering, *What the hell am I supposed to be doing in life?* She asks, "Do you have something you're working on right now? A project or something?"

I start to say, "I do some writing—" when she quickly interrupts with, "Yes! You have a book; no, you have a couple of books in you. You need to share it with the world!"

Maria went on to say, "I'm being told to tell you a story. It's a very old Persian story about a girl named Leila. The old woman guide wants me to tell you this." Suddenly, in my head, I'm hearing Eric Clapton singing Layla. I consider that I do want to make the best of this experience. I struggle to bring my mind back to the present moment; or maybe I've never really left it.

There were two young people very much in love but their parents wouldn't let them be together. The young man was in the desert sifting through the sand with his hands. When someone asked him what he was doing he answered he was looking for Leila. He was told, "Don't be foolish. Leila is not here in the sand." The young man answered, "Leila is everywhere. I hear her voice and I see her everywhere." He left the desert and went off until he came to a walled city. He hoped he might find her there. When he reached the gates, he found they had been locked for the night. He could not get inside, so he climbed the wall and jumped to the inside. His landing alerted the guards with their swords and a chase through the streets and alleys of the city began. He ran about not knowing where he was going or where any of the streets led. Finally he was facing another part of the city wall with the guards running toward him wielding their swords. He glanced about and realized he had no chance but to scale the wall. Somehow, as if by divine intervention, he was able to get his feet and hands on the stones of the wall and lifted himself upward to the top of the wall. He fell to the other side. Somewhat exhausted, but relieved and grateful for his freedom, he stood up and began to walk through this beautiful garden where he had landed. Ahead of him he saw a woman knelt over in the near darkness, looking for something she had lost in the grass. As he approached, she looked up. It was Leila. He ran toward her and fell to his knees embracing her. He said, I'd have kissed the blades of the swords had I known they were driving me to you.

"That's it! I was told to tell you that. I've never heard that story before in my life."

Somewhat startled and disbelieving, I ask, "You've never heard that story before?" As I was listening to her telling this tale, I had a vague awareness of this story's theme. I even had a flash of thinking it must be an older version of the Romeo and Juliet story.

She replies, "I've never heard that story before in my life! But she wanted me to tell it to you for some reason, so I repeated what she was saying to me."

Maria looks at me with a somewhat perplexed expression. She says, "You don't really have any idea; well, perhaps you've been aware of it a few times. But you really have no idea of the significance and transformative impact you have, and have had on the lives of so many people." I realize she is reading the puzzled look on my face. She continues, "It's not that you are doing anything in particular; the compassion and love that come through your vibration leaves such an impression. It transforms people and brings out the best in them."

She is so sincere. I feel speechless. I do manage to say, "That's a very nice compliment. Thank you."

She replies, "It's a very special and lovely gift that you bring to people. I smile as I stand up to leave. She says, "There is just one more thing I need to tell you."

I turn toward her and say, "Yes?"

She says, "2021 is going to be a most wonderful year for you; truly wonderful! You'll be walking on a path of sunlight."

As I walk away, Donna is coming forward for her reading. She tells me the one we both signed up for is almost ready for me. I am next on the list. I expected it to be a longer wait as there were several names ahead of mine. She assures me all the names are scratched out and mine is next. I wish Donna a good reading and head toward the psychic I am to see. I wish I had some time to reflect on the things Maria had said to me, but this next reader is calling out my name.

I'm unsure of what awaits me. There is a sense in me that this may be the frightened kind of experience anticipated by people who won't go to a psychic. I am surprised that this strange feeling has come over me. It is a hesitancy I have never felt before when going for a reading. Strange it is!

As I sit opposite this gypsy-looking woman, I notice two decks of cards laid out in two rows on the table in front of me. She smiles toward me and begins adjusting her long, black hair; pulling it up and saying no to herself. This hair play continues for a couple of minutes. She voices words such as, "up like this or down; bad breath, oh gum? Oh I'll have to write that down." She writes some words on a sheet of paper to her right. She keeps fooling with her hair and comments, "My spirits say things to me, but I don't know what I am supposed to do with my hair" as she looks directly at me for the first time. I'm sitting here thinking; *We've already used up some of my twenty-five minutes; and I can see that you are running late, possibly why people scratched off their names and left.*

Instead I say to her, "Sometimes I think I want to wear my hair up too." She asks me to turn on the recorder on my phone. I reply, "I'll remember better just by listening to what you say."

She seems to be taken aback and says, "Alright, if you'll remember it. I'm used to recording my readings. For twenty years I've always used tapes, and I'd give them to people. But now people use their phones." She is muttering again and fussing about the table and jotting words down on her paper. Finally she says, "Okay, I'll just have to begin the way I always do, so I can stay on track." She states her name, how long she has been a psychic, then she whispers to me, "What's your first name?" She continues, albeit with no recording device present, "This is a reading for Doreen," and finishes with the current date. She mutters something I can't distinguish, and tells me to pick a card from either of the decks. I choose a card and turn it over. It is a "Butterfly."

"Oh!" She sounds surprised. She proceeds to say, "The butterfly is a symbol of transformation and manifestation. It's the number one card. Get ready for a big breakthrough. Something you have manifested is coming." She then describes in her soft, rushed and panicky speech the caterpillar, the cocoon, the struggle to emerge and finally, the beautiful, colorful butterfly coming out. "Of course, she continues, "It can't fly right away. But the beautiful colors are all there. And, Oh, it's oh so beautiful!" She looks upward above her head as if a butterfly has just flown by us. I didn't see it. "So this means you are going through a transformation and something beautiful will be manifested in your life. But of course, this doesn't happen right away. I wanted this card pulled for a Yes or No answer. And it's upright, so it's a Yes." She doesn't tell me what the question is. The only question she posed to me was asking my first name. Is this an affirmation that I know my name? Perhaps she means that whatever question I have in mind would have a Yes answer. In my mind, I happen to be thinking, *Is this woman nuts?*

She directs me to pick up another card. I do. It is "Moose" #14. The card's message is: *Authority. You know what is best for you.* I smile and think, *Yes, and it certainly isn't this.*

I hear her say, "Moose! Moose spirit is very powerful. You know how a moose is. They're a big animal! If they walk out on the road in front of you: Well, you know…" She adjusts her body and raises her shoulders, as if to show me what a moose looks like. She continues, "But they stand so tall and are so graceful. When moose shows up, you're very powerful." She asks, "Do you have a question about another person?" I nod yes. "Pull a card for them," she says.

I choose a card and turn it over. It is "Deer" Gentle Pathfinder, # 41. It read, *Trust your instincts to guide you through this situation.* In addition to her panic, she seems baffled and dismayed now. The thought crosses my mind that these cards and messages are not conforming to what she wants to tell me, or what her spirits are telling her.

Based on her behavior, I am prepared to accept the messages on the cards, regardless of what her spirits might bring through. I am about to suggest that she and her spirits take a break; maybe go smoke a joint and chill.

She is saying the deer is very gentle and uses its senses and its light on its feet. Then she speaks about it being like an antelope that can outrun a lion because it is swift and agile and can make quick turns to the right or left. "Pick another card," she commands.

The card I pick is "Whale" #44 – Soul's Path. It reads, *Honor your soul's purpose.* Not only are the cards messages making some sense to me regarding my situation, but I am also drawn to the numbers on the cards. So far, I have turned over cards with the numbers one and four on them. Interesting, I think. All week I had been noticing these numbers on the clocks and in other places.

I hear her voice return with some mention of the "Whale" being my Destiny card. She is saying how the whale can breathe air but swims in the depths of the water; and this, she says, means I was on my right path. She points toward the cards for me to pick another.

I select and turn over "Snake." The card said *Healing: You are a healer.* The reader sounds enthusiastic at the sight of this card. It depicts an upright, standing cobra. She is saying that the snake can shed its skin and leave the old behind, as well as these parts, she points out, by the cobra's head, that help it capture its prey. It wasn't until this moment that I realized I had tuned her and her spirits out to attend to the cards myself. I don't really understand what she is referring to about the cobra, and decide not to ask for clarification.

I am recalling that in numerology the number one is symbolic of an independent spirit, manifestation and new beginnings; and the number four resonates with the vibrational energies of stability, practicality, organization, endurance and hard work. She hasn't mentioned anything about the numbers on the cards since the Butterfly which she pointed out was a number one. Without any further direction from her, I have been drawn to the numbers because of their frequent appearance in my day-to-day life recently.

Suddenly, something to my left catches my eye. I glance and see Donna looking at me; wanting to know how the reading is going; expecting me to give some visual cue only she could interpret. It is her turn next. I gave her a look adding the slightest, "NO," movement of my head.

I hear the psychic say, "Another one." I look at her and she is motioning me toward the row of cards. I pick the card "Antelope" and it reads, *Decisiveness: Make a decision and take appropriate action.*

I look at her and say, "That's funny. You were just speaking about the antelope." It's as though she isn't expecting this, and doesn't know what to say now.

She says, "Yes. It can move and turn very quickly." I wonder what that has to do with "decisiveness," but she is already telling me to pick one last card. This time she tells me to pick from the other deck. I select a card, "Spider" and it is in the reverse. The card says, Creativity. I don't read the rest as it is up-side-down. She tells me that a spider can make a web, and this means I am very creative and should be using my creative abilities. I wonder if its meaning is different in the reverse, but I won't ask.

She finishes by saying, "Well, that's your reading. Do you have any questions? I hope it was helpful."

My reply to her is, "You've had a busy day. Have you had a break?"

She answers, "No. Gum. I have to write that down. I'm going to the bathroom now." As I turn to leave, I think: *Good; because it seems you really need to!"*

Donna sees me approaching and walks over to meet me. I say, "Let's get out of here; you don't want to waste your money on her."

Donna says, "Yeah, I got the message! You didn't even have to move your head; your eyes said it all." On a cheerier note, she adds, "The reading I just had was excellent; and she told me I didn't need to go to any other reader's in here because they were all going to give me the same messages. She said I wasn't going to hear anything different than what she had just told me." I look at her and wish I had been told that. But I knew I probably wouldn't have listened.

Witnessed

It has been said that life does not give us what we deserve but what we negotiate. The word negotiate may sound like discussing something, but it is a way to come to an agreement or get around a difficult situation. It may include a silent acceptance; not unlike an agreement in absentia. This comes to mind as I began reading today's obituaries. I still like reading the morning paper and still check out the obituaries. My father used to say that he read the obituaries to see if he was in there. I read obituaries because they intrigue me. They reveal a great deal, both by what is said and what is left unsaid; what is included or missed. This morning's paper carried the obituary of a man I knew. In fact, I know this family well, and I am very fond of them. It must be difficult to report the passing of a loved one, and try to embody in a few paragraphs the gregarious life of such a renaissance man. He had intellect, confidence and skills allowing him to do most anything. He also carried a boldness and a physique that enabled him to be a dominant presence in any room, organization, and in the family home. In many respects it captured the public persona and the outgoing, personal characteristics of this God-fearing man. Some, who knew him well, might read those words and say,

If I'd done some of the things he's done, I'd fear God too! Others, more generous souls, might suggest; *He was a good Christian who made sure Jesus didn't die for nothing.* About ten years ago, an old friend of mine refused to go to any more funerals or read any more obituaries because he said he didn't know who they were talking about; No one ever described the scoundrel he had known. Respect for the dead, and for the life that no longer advances among us tends to be expected in obituaries, and rightly so, for we want to recall the goodness and love their soul embodied, their essence, and set aside our judgements.

At a time when nothing physical remains, it does seem appropriate to ignore any misdeeds of the dead. All potentiality has departed. But those who loved them will try to remember the goodness and laughter they brought to the world. People will share their happy memories, and try to keep those aspects alive. Lying, cheating, stealing, manipulation, molestation, in fact, any and all transgressions of the Ten Commandments, must be laid to rest. But one does wonder if these silences make us moral cowards. Personal or family pain can seep into society and take deeper roots, gaining strength and control through powerful positioning. Some say silence is golden. Golden or not, there are times silence needs to be broken. Things grow in silence. In his acceptance speech for the Nobel Peace Prize, Elie Wiesel (Dec. 1986) reminded us to not be silent. Those who want to be bullies are helped by our silence. Our silence becomes our placid acceptance of wrong-doing. We are not helping those who are wronged by keeping silent about the bullying. There are consequences to behaviors, and silence is a behavior. These effects live on long after the deeds may be forgotten, forgiven or revenged. Six decades after the Women's Movement we are living in a time of the 'Me Too' movement partly because women have been silent, but mainly because men and women have faltered in their own self-respect. Racial hatred, predominately and shamefully exhibited six decades ago, grew silent but did not stop. People silently pretended it wasn't there. It just silently continued to live on, and today, we are still having to proclaim the obvious: Black Lives Matter. A truth subjugated mainly by those meant to serve us. In this same period of time we have progressed in leaps and bounds technologically, yet, we have not, with all the means afforded us, curbed hatred and abuse. The dominance of world religions for thousands of years has not unified people, but stirred more hatred and division, although that is not what they proclaim. Revolutions, wars, peace marches, demands for tolerance and acceptance have not moved us, as human beings, to accept a basic truth: *There is no one greater or lesser than I am.* I will treat others the way I want them to treat me. Having different circumstances does not change truth. How difficult can that concept be to grasp and put into practice? It takes a will to make the way! It's not unlike wearing a mask during a pandemic; everyone must be committed to doing it for the greater good: to prevent the spread of dis-ease among us.

Could this not be the ideal we all seek; to care for ourselves and one another? It begins and ends with each person. It seems to me that the respect and honoring of our essence, our goodness, is what we pay tribute to at life's end. We all embody this treasure, this spirit of goodness to express in life. Whether we choose to do so or not, we can be sure that when the body is gone, so, too, is this potential. It has nothing left to embody it. Why do we waste it, when we only have this life to express our goodness to ourselves and others?

Instead of respecting ourselves and our own dignity and goodness, and seeing and honoring that dignity and goodness in the other, we treat life like a playground for negotiations. Life becomes a place where we watch our negotiations unfold, most often, without boundaries of self-respect in place. In death, it seems we are all as innocent as we are guilty. Whatever our misdeeds, brought about by our failure to respect one another, they are buried with us. At last, that which was innocent and truthful is honored as it leaves its embodiment.

While this obituary has triggered these reflections, it has also drawn my attention to what is expected but absent in this announcement. I noticed, unlike what I had seen in other obituaries, the maiden name of his widow was not included. This seemed to stand out among the things missing. It led me to wonder if all those she knew would recognize her loss. Who is this woman who has lost her beloved husband? Without her maiden name given, it seems she is to be identified through her husband. The maiden name for the mother of the recently departed, a woman who died many years ago, was reported. This, I suppose, would identify his ancestry and the quality of his lineage. However, the ancestry of his living wife, who contributed to the quality of his life, seemed to be overlooked. She had a full name once. It left me with a foreboding sense that she, like her name, had somehow been lost. I will name her: Judy Harmon.

He was introduced to me many years ago by Judy, the woman he married. She was a shy, intelligent and beautiful girl who would be his wife for fifty-seven years before this departure. This young, Catholic, country girl, with her coquettish quietness and beauty seemed to suit him and meet his needs as much as his flamboyant confidence and devil-may-care youthfulness seemed to balance her need for a strong masculine energy she could rely upon to fulfill her. Judy began dating him when she was eighteen, and they married when she was nineteen. He was nearly twenty-four and had already lived and worked in the city Ten months after their wedding, their first child was born. They would have three more children to complete their beautiful family.

Once while she was at home with three young preschoolers, two in diapers, a friend came to visit. It was observed that Judy was a busy mother but somewhat disorganized in her day. Necessity had not yet encouraged her to be in charge of how her day would flow. She said she wanted to make a cake for supper, and her friend offered to do that with the packaged mix that she had on hand. When they finished lunch with the children, the cake was mixed and poured into the pans. Just then her husband arrived home, not for lunch, but because he was driving by and decided to stop in. He commented on the cakes going into the oven and immediately began to lose his mind over how much batter remained on the beaters. He shouted about how much batter was being wasted and that only half the cake was being baked. While Judy smiled shyly, her friend assured the husband that the batter had been tapped off the beaters and the cake would turn out just fine. He continued to shake his head about the waste, hugged the children and said he had to get back to work. He left. At dinnertime, he arrived home and noticed the table was not set. The women were busy getting dinner ready to be served. He took plates from the cupboard and began tossing them around the table. When his wife's friend got the cutlery and continued with setting the table, he sat on a kitchen chair and began reading the paper. The effort toward setting the table seemed, not so much to be helpful but, a demonstration of what he expected to see done. When the double-layer chocolate cake with chocolate icing was served, he gave a loud, hearty laugh about how the cake looked and said that if all the batter had been put into it, it might have raised higher and looked like a real cake. Judy spoke his name, as if to get him to stop. His perception of how the cake looked did not prevent him from eating a generous portion. Rather than acknowledge his earlier rudeness or apologize for it, he continued to expand it, in spite of the contrary evidence. The friend silently wondered if this was how he treats his wife, and if he was a helicopter husband. She believed it must be typical due to the placid tolerance of Judy regarding his behavior toward her friend.

From the missing information, in this obituary, I am brought to an awareness of a likeness I now see, for the first time, between this widow, Judy, and her mother. During all the years I have known her, I did not notice this; had not made this connection. Perhaps I had always been looking for what was more obvious like the smile, the nose, the eyes, to appreciate a resemblance. The traits caught through a way of being, rather than looking, are not as immediately evident. There is an old expression about behavior: "it's easier caught than taught." It means we learn and do things that are not specifically "taught" to us, like standing at the sink and putting one foot on top of the other. No one teaches you to do that, you just "catch" it; you pick it up. What's missing seems to trigger this realization.

It was just a few months before her eighteenth birthday, I recall, when Judy's mother passed away. I remember being surprised, at the time, that her mother's obituary was only a couple of lines stating she had died and where and when her burial would take place. It did not state her own name; only that she was "Mrs." followed by her husband's name. In her case, not only was her maiden name excluded but her very own identification, the name given to her by her parents, was not included. Perhaps it was my indoctrination into the women's movement of the 1960s that had peaked my awareness of this omission. At the time, I went searching through other obituaries in the newspaper to see if all women were treated this way. I knew with my feisty spirit and the women's movement behind me, this would have to change. To my surprise and relief, I found this identification of women was not the norm. I cringed at the thought of it being disrespectful. After all, this was not a disrespectful family. Could it be, that in someone's thinking, her stature came from being someone's wife? Indeed, a good wife of a good man.

Yet, today, I still shiver at such a concept. A silencing of her personhood.

The way Judy and her mother lived their lives was different. Truly, different generations with different expectations. The similarity was more in the way they allowed themselves to be treated by others. Their husbands were very different. Her husband professed his dominance;

he always knew best and was sure he was always right. It seemed he could assess for timidness or a lack of self-respect. If that is what he found, you could be vulnerable prey. Judy's father, her mother's husband, was a gentle man, considerate of others' opinions, hardworking, and one of the faithful. There appeared to be more of a balanced relationship between her parents even though the cultural norms of their generation would have allowed for male dominance.

During her life Judy had many health concerns: loss of a kidney, knee replacements, skin cancer and lived on a regime of anti-inflammatories. Her self-care did not include daily exercise. By her late sixties, Judy had reached the point of immobility and had to rely on walkers and wheelchairs. Once her sister was asked to accompany her to a medical appointment, to check her hearing, at the hospital. A family member had to be with her because of her compromised mobility, and her husband and children were unable to help her on that particular day. Previously, she had been prescribed hearing aids after it was determined she did not have wax build-up in her ears. After testing and try-outs, she finally got hearing aids but she still could not hear with them. The hearing specialist requested that she see a doctor at the hospital. The appointment came while Judy was in rehab for her mobility issues. At the hospital a nurse led them to the doctor's office. Soon the doctor entered. He spoke loudly, and Judy indicated she could hear him. He looked in her ears and said she had fluid in both ears and told her they would have to be drained before he could accurately evaluate her hearing. She listened intently. The doctor then suggested he could put tubes in her ears immediately so the fluid could drain or make another appointment for her to come back later. Judy couldn't decide what to do. Her sister, Valerie, asked if it was the same procedure that's done for children when they have tubes put in their ears. The doctor announced, "Exactly the same. It only takes five minutes." Judy made no comment. The doctor stood up and said he'd be back in a few minutes for her answer, and that he could do the procedure within the next fifteen minutes if she chose to do it. He left the room. Judy was silent.

Valerie said, "My kids had tubes put in their ears as there was fluid that made it hard for them to hear, and they were fine after that was done.

Judy replied, "Well I don't know what I should do."

Valerie asked, "Do you want to be able to hear?"

"Oh, yes! More than anything," Judy replied.

Valerie asked, "Do you want that to happen today, or do you want to make another appointment and come back another time?

Judy answered, "I don't want to come back for any more appointments."

Valerie said, "Then you'll have to tell the doctor what you want. Speak up for yourself!" It almost seemed as if Judy expected everyone else to know what she wanted or needed or that they would figure it out, and then tell her what was going to happen. She would not have to be accountable for any decisions or outcomes. Compliance was all she seemed to expect of herself. Perhaps, seeing and relying upon doctors for so many years, convinced her "doctors know best."

The doctor came into the office saying, "Well, have you decided?" Judy glanced at her sister. Valerie knew who had to remain silent and who had to speak. The doctor sat in front of Judy and said, "I have a few minutes right now to do it. I'd just have to go get tubes and make sure the room is ready."

Judy shook her head yes and uttered, "Let's do it."

The doctor said, "Follow me next door." Judy smiled toward her sister with a look of pride. Valerie pushed her in her wheelchair into the next room. The doctor helped her get up onto the bed. He left and came back in a couple of minutes and did the procedure. He told her to just lay there a few minutes before getting up. She was still prone when he returned.

He asked, "How does that feel?"

Judy answered, "Great! Can you do the other one, too?" He seemed surprised and asked, "You want the other one done? Yeah, I'll do it! I'll be right back." He left, returned with more tubes and did the procedure on the other ear. He helped her sit up and get back in her wheelchair. On the tunneled walk back to the rehab center, Judy seemed blissful. She kept saying, "Oh, it is so good to hear again." It seemed silence had been unmasked in more ways than one for her. That must have felt delightful.

If memory serves me well, Judy's older sister, Eve, did not have the warmest relationship with their mother. They seemed to have very different personalities. Eve, who would never consider herself a feminist, drove a vehicle, helped her husband in his business and cared for her home and children with nurturance. She would voice her opinion and take a stand for the under-dog. Eve seemed to view their mother as too timid and compliant; a woman who rarely ever left her home although she cared for many including visitors and the friends of her children. Eve could not see the quiet strength that others saw in her mother. One could get the impression that Eve viewed her mother as passive and too accepting of all that came her way. Yet, they were both practical women. The mother's practicality, derived more out of financial necessity, and Eve, maybe, had grown practical because she had caught the concept of "waste not, want not." She certainly did not get the concept of "burning your bra" as anything but waste of a perfectly good undergarment. Her admiration for her father, however, was noticeable. He seemed to embody more of a balance of both the masculine and feminine energies. He worked away from home and provided the income for the family. When he was home, usually just on the week-ends, he was nurturing and loving toward his wife and children. I don't think he ever cooked a meal for himself. He was waited on. In those days, that seemed to be the expectation as well as a sign of a devoted wife. Eve liked to dote on him, too. A devoted wife-in-training, but with a mind of her own.

When Eve heard of the engagement of her younger sister, Judy, I realized that she was not impressed to have that man as her brother-in-law. Her objection was not stated directly but rather in reflection or deflection to their dead mother. The comment spoken was, "Mother would turn in her grave." I had never heard that expression before but it certainly conveyed an energy of arousal. Nothing more was said. Perhaps, though, she had some knowledge or awareness of her mother's values or opinions; and that she might protest about something she didn't agree with. An indication that she knew her mother wasn't docile. Throughout the years, however, Eve's fondness grew for her brother-in-law. She liked his assertiveness and take-charge attitude. At the same time, Eve showed disappointment that her encouragement toward her sister, Judy, to engage more in the activities of daily life, fell on an energy of passivity.

In reflection, it seems an inherent characteristic of the women in the Harmon family was one of pleasing others. Generally, being a pleaser is rewarded with smiles and thanks and praises. But not pleasing? Well, that may be determined by the style of the one not pleased and their level of feeling offended or entitled. It might manifest itself as a frown, name-calling, or humiliation in front of others. In violent families, it may even be darker. Like all behaviors, it has a purpose. It not only expresses disapproval, but it asserts the dominance of the one who is to be pleased. It develops one's sense of value and worth. It works to create a broken-spirit, reduce confidence, and further silence the timid. You either learn to pick your fights or you don't fight or stand up for yourself at all. Behaviors are a silent form of negotiation. Pleasing others is a fine characteristic to learn and practice, if it does not run amuck. Like anger, or any emotion or behavior, it must be tempered. It must send the correct message.

There is a day or time, I believe, when our pleasing, or any excess, is tested. It happens, I suppose, to help us identify the demarcation of where we need to learn to draw the line. In regard to pleasing, I suspect the testing happens when you still know your worth, and know that you matter, too; when it is still a fairly level playing field. If you realize that anything or everything about your worth is at stake, there can be no passivity and no wavering in your negotiation.

Such a situation occurred with Judy's younger sister, Valerie. She, too, was a pleaser. Valerie seemed to overlook many dismissive or degrading behaviors directed toward her. It seemed as if those things didn't bother her. But that one day came. Was it a day of escalation or a day of reckoning? Who knows? It was a day she would not accept an abusive response to her pleasing efforts. It was a day she knew her worth, and the goodness in her soul. Valerie did not know the black feminist and activist, June Jordan, who was determined to treat herself well. She did not know how important it would be to have the self-love and self-respect that Jordan demanded for herself. Yet, somewhere, in the unity of souls where dignity, righteousness and freedom exist, where there is no division, she acted from this same knowing of truth.

It was the time her husband wouldn't eat her tuna casserole. Valerie knew he did not like tuna sandwiches, or at least, thought he didn't, as he always refused to eat one. Her friends and neighbors often made tuna casseroles for dinner and their husbands and children enjoyed them. She thought she would try making one. It smelled wonderful baking in the oven. The table was set and the children were hungry to eat when their father got home. He walked into the kitchen smiling and offering his usual embrace and kiss. A scene his children had often witnessed. As the children were taking their places at the table, he asked, "What's for supper?"

Valerie answered, "Tuna casserole."

His mood changed and he said, "I'm not eating that!" She said, "Well, surely you can try it. It smells good!" He washed his hands and reluctantly sat into the table. The casserole was served. He took one taste and shoved his plate toward the center of the table. He scowled, "That's not fit to eat!" Everyone took notice.

Valerie looked at him and said, "They were all good ingredients. I don't serve you food that is not fit to eat." Two of the children shoved their plates aside and said they didn't like it. They asked for a sandwich.

Valerie would not admonish their father in front of them; but, by the look on her face, she was more than "not impressed" with his behavior. She said to the children, "This casserole is made with tuna, and you all like tuna, so eat your supper."

Their father interjected with, "Don't make them eat that. Get them a sandwich, and don't ever make this again!" Valerie got up from the table and went to the kitchen counter with her back to them. For a few seconds, she stood there in disbelief. She had never witnessed nor experienced anything like this from him in their twelve years together. She could not believe what she had just seen and heard. In a stunned state, she told herself to do something; don't just stand there. As she reached to get peanut butter out of the cupboard, she felt his hand on her shoulder. Valerie turned toward him, suppressing the rage that was rising up inside her, and whispered, "Don't." He slapped her across the face with his right hand. The action further stunned her long enough to momentarily suppress the mounting rage. She glanced toward the children and noticed one had seen this, and her mind took a snapshot of the fear on her son's face.

Valerie left the kitchen and hurried upstairs. Her mind raced through so many scenarios of what she would and would not do during those few seconds it took her to reach their bedroom. She had been filled with sorrow in her life; and she had been filled with joy in her life; but she had never before experienced every recess of her body being filled with rage. It was then, he walked into the bedroom and said, "Come on. Come on downstairs." The rage had her trembling, and it was all she could do to control it.

Valerie took a step toward him, and never took her eyes off his as she said, "Don't you ever, ever do that to me again or I will kill you." The idea of the size of her up against the size of him, and perhaps the thought of "you're beautiful when you're angry," made him do another foolish thing. He allowed a trace of a smirk to appear on his face. Gas on her fire. Valerie raised her hand pointing her finger at him and said, "This is not funny. I mean it. I will kill you or you will kill me because I will not stop until one of us is dead. The other one will be going to prison, and those kids downstairs will be going to Child Protection. Don't you think for one second that I will be running to women's shelters to protect myself from some fucking bastard who thinks he has some right to abuse me. I am NEVER living my life that way! You just modeled for your son how to be a wife abuser. Is that what you want for him?"

Valerie saw him soften as understanding and compassion filled his eyes. He said, "Oh honey. I'm so sorry!" She was able to control her voice enough to say to him what needed to be said, but she could not control the rage in her eyes, and he saw it. It was a time that called for language that would be irrevocably understood.

She stepped back and said, "Don't you fuckin' sorry me! I don't care if you're sorry. This is your one and only warning: If you ever lay an unkind hand on me again, it will be the end of this family." Again, he took a step toward her, to comfort her this time, to seek forgiveness, but, in that moment, this did not seem a forgivable offence. Valerie said, "Don't you touch me. You better get downstairs and see that those kids are okay." Whatever had been negotiated up to that moment had just been clarified.

"Will you come down? Please come down," he begged.

She said, "I'll come down when I'm ready." It took her a few minutes to calm herself enough to go back downstairs where the children were. They had left the table and had gone about their activities. He never physically mistreated her again. She never made a tuna casserole again. It left a bad taste in her mouth. She loved him enough to give him a warning. He loved her enough and, perhaps, himself enough to never cross that line again. But mostly, she loved herself enough to make her boundaries clear to both of them.

My mind returns to the obituary, and to this family now mourning their loss. After their family grew, they sold their city home and built a house in the country, a couple of hours to drive there, and they would spend the next twenty years living there. They would meet new neighbors and friends. The Church always served as a congregation of like-minded, and still enables people to connect with one another. Winters could be harsh, so they travelled South before the first snowfall and returned in April. The trips South had to stop because of Judy's declining health and mobility issues. His efforts to care for her at home began to take its toll on his own health as they aged. Judy agreed to live in a Nursing Home where the care she needed would be provided around the clock. He would visit her daily as their home was nearby. He spoke of friends and neighbors visiting him and bringing him food; no doubt, a treat, as he had been doing most of the cooking and housework himself for many years. They would ask about his wife and how she was doing. Judy had been in the nursing home for just over a year. He had fallen a few times, and this prompted him to get a walker for support.

Then the Coronavirus pandemic hit and a lockdown occurred. From March until June the residents of nursing homes could have no visitors. This was to keep them from contracting the virus, and spreading it among the other residents. This meant he could not visit her. They spent their fifty-seventh wedding anniversary apart but, thanks to technology, they were able to see and talk to each other through FaceTime. As restrictions were about to lift in late June, he was rushed to the hospital and underwent emergency surgery for bowel perforations. This was followed by another surgery a week later. His recovery was fluctuating, and he was in and out of the intensive care unit. Family and friends were asked to pray for him and his recovery. They did. Progress was noted. Judy was happily anticipating a visit from him as soon as he was well enough to be discharged as social distancing restrictions had been lifted for family visits. This was not to be. His condition worsened and he passed away.

On Saturday, the daughter, of Judy and her deceased husband, sent a message to an uncle and asked that it be circulated to other family members. It stated that due to the pandemic and social distancing requirements, it had been negotiated with medical offices and the nursing home to have Judy attend the funeral, and have a final good-bye. This meant that the terms of the negotiation limited the funeral to just his widow and children. It would be a private family affair. A text was sent at noon on Monday to one of the children confirming the definition of family as wife and children only. He had died on Wednesday morning, and his obituary appeared in the paper for the first time on Monday morning. This delay was because arrangements had to be made and negotiated with the nursing home and covid medical offices to have Judy attend the funeral. In the reply, the child confirmed that "family" meant wife and children only; and also forwarded the message that had been sent previously to the uncle. It stated they were glad they inherited their father's negotiating skills and had been able to arrange for their mother to attend her husband's funeral with them. There was no date or time mentioned in the obituary, only the name of his final resting place. He would be laid to rest in the cemetery of his childhood community. Since no one was allowed to attend, there was no need to announce the date or time in the paper. Hence, the reason that information was missing from his obituary.

It is now Wednesday; a week since his passing, and two days after reading his obituary. It is the day of his funeral. Another friend of that family had been speaking to one of the pallbearers, a nephew of the deceased who had been summoned by the funeral director to help carry the coffin. Not seeing his aunt Judy enter the Church, this nephew asked Judy's son if she had arrived yet. He was told, "She's not coming. At eleven o'clock Monday morning the Nursing Home called and told us they wouldn't let her come." Silence about this change had been maintained. The remaining family had not been notified or told that they could now attend the funeral. The son then continued saying, "You know, I thought there would be more people here than this."

Shocked, the pallbearer-cousin replied, "But everyone was told not to come!"

The son replied, "We didn't think anyone would pay attention to that." A jaw-dropper to the uninitiated. Disturbing behaviors that evoke silence.

It reminds me of what Carl G. Jung said about the ridiculous and wildly unreasonable lengths people will go to avoid facing themselves. We will not become self-aware until we look within, and bring our own darkness into the light of awareness.

Let Us Remember

At the top of the stairs in our family home hung a bright blue sturdy cardboard plaque with the verse:

> *Only one life*
> *Twill soon be past*
> *Only what's done*
> *For Christ will last*
> *(C.T. Studd, 1860–1931)*

It was there in plain sight but, like many messages, it carried more of a subliminal quality that could influence our lives. The message that may fall below our threshold of consciousness is not that life is short but that there are only certain things we do that really matter. Those are the things done for Christ, "the anointed one."

As a child, the younger siblings, including me, were willingly brought to our little mission church, Saint Martin's Roman Catholic Church every Sunday. Our dad, who was only home for that one full day of the week, saw the wisdom in ending his work week and beginning his day of rest by gathering his children and attending morning Mass. Some of the older children, who were not always so willing, were not forced to go; that would have been counter-intuitive. Nevertheless, he continued to set an example of what he believed was the right thing to do. We always sat to the right facing the altar, in the first pew, to ensure we were not distracted and could remain focused on the Mass. If we were to look behind us, and we did, we were given a glance and a movement of the head that said, "turn around." Symbolic information and gestures spoke to us.

Almost sixty years later, my memories return me to those days. The last Mass ever to be held at Saint Martin's Roman Catholic Church occurs today, August 29, 2020. There will be no fanfare. It is just the regular Sunday Mass. But it is the closing of the church that stirs these feelings and memories. St. Martin's has embraced the presence of all those Catholics who built it, and lived and grew in its surrounding communities. Those who have been laid to rest around this structure remain gathered for the good-bye. For more than one hundred and sixty years, the living congregated there as a community of believers giving thanks and adoration to the God who lived and lives within them. In that little space they gathered to recognize and celebrate their Oneness in God.

For some of the more senior residents of the congregation, I know there is lamentation. Their hearts are broken at the loss of their little church and of no longer being able to attend Mass there. At this farewell, St. Martins and all it has meant will be celebrated in the hearts, minds and souls of each of us wherever we are. There is a sense, however, that the leave-taking of this place holds almost more importance than the Mass itself. I sometimes wonder about the discernment of our memories and what it is we hold as meaningful and important. I had planned to be there today, now I feel torn as to whether or not I want to go. It feels like a funeral of sorts: A time to say good-bye to a past, a childhood, and a way of life that is no more. This stirs thoughts of scripture:

When I was a child, I spoke as a child; I felt as a child; I thought as a child. Now that I have become a man, I have put away childish things. (1 Corinthians 13:11; The World English Bible, WEB, @ bible.org).

Always a reminder to me that growth itself requires that we release the past and move forward. Writing this quote, I notice the language has been modernized, but the word "man" is not changed to "adult." Could this suggest an unconscious energy resisting integration of the feminine?

Saint Martin's is a part of my past, but its existence, presence and influence in my life, and in the lives of thousands of men, women and children will remain. But for how long? How long will there be a memory of the existence of this place? There is still a graveyard that surrounds the church where the faithful and devoted souls are gathered to remain in peace. The granite stones that mark their places signify that they will always be remembered. I am confused by this foreboding feeling that wants to keep me away. I think it may be a fear that I will form a memory of an insensitive dismissal by a priest just doing his duty, someone who has no memories of this place or its soulfulness to the rest of us.

Perhaps I will go there today, but not in person. I will go in my imagination and memories, for that is the only way that will remain for me to ever go there again. Yes, that is what I will do.

In my imagination, I have parked the car and now stand here on this church property. Before I make my way through those doors ahead of me, doors I've walked through many times, I linger at the outskirts of the cemetery where there once stood a fence and gate. Here lies numerous, unbaptized infants in graves that were left unmarked. Each one of them had a name because their mothers who labored to give them life also named them, as if to summon them forth. Only in the past few years did a stone appear "outside the gate." A marker insisted upon by a mother as she neared her own death. A mother, like all the other mothers, who had been haunted all of her life by the lack of acknowledgement of her firstborn infant and the little soul's displacement by her religious community. How does one reconcile that behavior with the agape of Christ? Baptism, a rite of admission and adoption by the Church, also carries the belief that babies are tainted by original sin and this must be washed away by the waters of baptism. This is not a personal sin or wrong-doing, but a sin, we are told, that has been transmitted to all the descendants of Adam and Eve, mythical figures, from generation to generation at birth. As a child I learned that original sin was the disobedience of Adam and Eve to God's command to "not eat from the tree of the knowledge of good and evil." They were created in God's image, and this act of disobedience was hubristic resulting in God throwing them out of the Garden of Eden. That's the story I was told.

Another feature that seems important to be remembered about baptism is that during this Rite, the individual is also anointed with oil. Being anointed with oil was an ancient practice bestowed on kings and priests and symbolized they were "chosen ones." Just as Christ (Christos) is the anointed or chosen one, so are we anointed at baptism.

In truth, we know these babies conceived in love and nurtured in the womb are never forgotten because they, too, are children of God. In the biblical psalms we are told that God will never forget us no matter what; and as Elie Wiesel pointed out, God remembers. That's why he's God. We have been repeatedly reminded through our faiths, our religions and throughout our lives of the importance of memory. "Only what's done for Christ will last," is a reminder. We are to remember that. We have been taught in the Christian tradition that Jesus, at the Last Supper, after he had given thanks, and broke the bread said, "This is my body that is for you. Do this in remembrance of me." We hear these words spoken every day at Mass. This same message is presented to modern generations through epic tales, theatre and animated cinema such as in The Lion King. We are reminded that we are able to take our rightful place in life if we will remember who we are.

I suddenly recall a story once told to me by a Hindu friend; perhaps because of its likeness to the Adam and Eve story: According to an ancient Hindu legend, she said, there was once a time when all human beings were gods; but because they abused their divinity, Brahma, the chief god, decided to take it away from them and hide it where it could never be found. All the gods met to decide where that secret place would be. They could not think of any place on earth where it could be hidden and not found.

Then, Brahma said, "Here is what we will do, we will hide their divinity deep within the center of their own being for humans will never think to look for it there." All the gods agreed this was the perfect hiding place; and the deed was done. Ever since then, humans have been searching for something already within themselves.

The message is similar to one C.G. Jung quotes from the 41st letter of Seneca (4bce-65ce) to Lucillius (Gummere trans., pp.272–273) in C.G. Jung, CW, Vol. 5, Symbols of Transformation, p.78. Seneca suggests that outward expressions of prayer aren't necessary because God's spirit lives within us. We need to go within to connect with and have a relationship with the divine. He suggests we can seek our permission from this divine inner source.

I meander toward the steps and open one of the double doors to the church entry. This addition occurred during my youth. It wasn't always here. The double doors were opened at funerals to get the coffin in and out. I slowly walk up the aisle to the front pew. In my earliest years here the inside of this church was a neutral light beige color that drew no attention to itself. One's focus was always drawn to the altar, even for the priest whose back was always to the congregation. Things changed. In the mid-1960s, Mass was said, for the first time, in English instead of Latin, and the priest faced the people. A great deal was lost and unseen in that change of perspective. For many years the inside of this church has been this sky-blue color with painted brown pews. I never liked it. These colors feel like they belong in a cathedral with frescas and many stained-glass windows. It made this little church feel like something it's not. It is a small, humble structure and in its simplicity and purity invited and welcomed the presence of Christ. It was enough.

In my imagination, I genuflect before the altar. As I enter the pew and kneel for a prayer, I think of the many young men and women in love who once knelt before this altar and committed their lives to each other in the Sacrament of Matrimony, a physical manifestation of God's grace, blessing them so they may experience the divine in their union. The priest, the congregation, even the building itself bore witness to their consecration. Maybe that is why it feels important to return to these physical places.

My husband and I were not married here, but in a chapel not much larger than this mission church. The year my husband passed away, to mark the memory of our wedding day and what would have been our forty-seventh anniversary, I decided to visit the chapel where we had been married. It was at the Catholic university where I had been a student. I walked up those steps and went inside to the main entrance of the building that once housed administration, and the dorm I called home for a time. Another set of steps stood before me. I once walked up those steps with my dad who was prepared to give his youngest daughter away in marriage to a man he felt was worthy of her. That memory was jolted the moment I opened the chapel door. I stood there in disbelief. The aisle I had walked down with my dad was now a corridor with computers and desks on either side. There was no altar, just a bare, neutral wall before me. An employee of the university walked by and asked if I was alright. Apparently, I was visibly shaken. I muttered that I had just come to visit the chapel. She said, "We don't have a chapel here anymore. There's a meditation room up on the second floor. If you want to go there, I'll show you where it is."

I answered, "No. No, I don't want to go there." Maybe it was that experience, or the memory of it, that tugs at me today. Perhaps it is less shocking and easier to release something when we know this is the end; it will be no more. But to find something gone that you expect to see again can stun. The shock value may be related to the sudden death of a friend you had dinner with last night compared to the death of a friend who is on life support in the hospital. An expectation somehow dulls the shock and loss.

Is there a value to being in the presence, one last time, of where our memories were made? Surely, the last time I was there was the last time. But then, there was no talk of closing the church. Regardless, from that moment on, I have only memory; and there will be no new memories to make here. I am miles away from St. Martin's, at this moment, but I hold it in my imagination and in my memory. I imagine how the church is starting to fill up with some familiar faces and with some unknown faces who have graced the building during the years I have been away. While waiting for the priest to arrive I would want to turn around, smile and nod to those I know. If I was in that front pew, I would be focused on the Mass once it began. But I sit at home and it makes no difference to my mind that wants to wander. Although wandering does not mean I am lost, I am beginning to feel lost in my thoughts.

I am taken back to that same day I couldn't find the chapel to reconnect with my past. I recall making my way outside, with something of a stagger, and sitting in my car. I felt unable to move. Suddenly, I was overcome with thoughts of extinction. I recalled that in two different cities where my children had been born, the hospitals where I gave birth to them had been imploded. I had lost my husband. I was his "Mrs." and now I am nobody's. When we lose our belonging to anything or anyone, it is a desolate feeling. It may be part of the reason we must remember.

These are curious times for it seems to me people don't exercise their memories well. They rely on others or machines to perform that function for them: Alexa, Siri or cell phones. Some don't trust anyone with an intact memory because to them it is just as elusive as magic. Those who are rarely present in the moment and do not reflect on what they see or hear make strange claims about memory. While they give little to no focus to their own experiences, they seem to have no trouble in telling others that their memories are bullshit and didn't even happen. It is one thing to be oblivious to your own life, but to suggest to another that their experiences and memories did not occur is atrocious. I can only think that such behavior is designed to steal your truth and pull you into a shadowy world of confusion and doubt. It may be a reflection of their lives, but it is not your life. When you have lived it, you know it. Remember it.

In his acceptance speech for the Nobel Peace Prize, Elie Wiesel (1986) spoke of the importance of remembering. His profound insight, undoubtedly grew from his strong Jewish faith and his horrific experiences and loses during the Holocaust and his subsequent efforts to try to understand those experiences. Yet his awareness of the importance of healing and his struggle to do so informed him that we must not remember with hatred and revenge in our hearts. Those feelings must be released so they do not dominate our memories and hope for humankind.

I have personal memories of influential experiences that shaped my life. Once, when I was a young girl, I left my class notes in school and I had to study for a test. My dad was amused at my distress. He thought if I had written the notes down, then I should remember them. He continued to explain that when he was a child in the early 1920s, a hundred years ago now, each child had a slate and each lesson was written on it with chalk. When it was time for the next lesson, you had to erase your slate and copy the next lesson on it. A slate was about the size of a modern-day Kindle or small iPad. The lesson remained on the slate until you erased it, and with a slate, when you erased it, it was gone for good. The only back-up was your memory. You had to rely on yourself. Memorization was important. It was the "use it or lose it" concept. The same concept that has been applied in the decision to close smaller churches. What we don't use, we will lose! At age ninety, my dad could still recite Robert Service's, "The Cremation of Sam McGee." It always gave him and his listeners great pleasure. Some of the verses are timeless and remain metaphorically true:

There are strange things done in the midnight sun
By the men who moil for gold
The Arctic trails have their secret tales
That would make your blood run cold...
(Robert Service, 1907)

There are some long-time parishioners who have felt that the closing of St. Martin's has made their blood run cold. The church was part of their own tradition and an icon in their lives. Whether it is true or not, some believe that the church was inconsiderately and underhandedly eclipsed from their lives. These feelings are often part of the anger that accompany the emotional process of loss. This church closing will be an intimate experience for each of us because it was not only a building that witnessed our lives, our confessions, our prayers and our promises; but what took place within its walls and within each of us is what is really important. Let us remember, this church was built as a place to bring the Mass to the people.

Like prior generations, many of us made our First Communion in this little church with all those we saw every Sunday gathered round us. It was a Rite of Passage where, at about age seven, we could join the adults in receiving the Eurchrist: The Body of Christ. As if any of us knew what that really meant. What was conveyed to us and understood by us was simply this: **It's very important!** For some, a trust and faith in that message would suffice. For others, becoming adults and putting away the things of childhood, might enable deeper understanding through reflection and learning. Unfortunately for many, the Mass would be regarded as merely a symbolic replication of the Last Supper. I think today, as this church is closed, we must not forget the importance of the Mass, and why this building was erected and brought into existence in the first place.

Carl G. Jung (1875–1961, Psychoanalyst) explains that the Catholic Mass is **so important** because Christ is always present in the Mass. He references the Catholic doctrine of *Transubstantiation* (which was reinstated by Pope Paul VI in the encyclical Mysterium fidei in 1965) that speaks of the literal presence of Christ in the Eucharist, even though there is no physical change in the appearance of the bread or wine. He notes that Christ's presence, as a literal truth, is essential to the Mystery. Jung explains that in the Mass the words of the Sanctus suggest that the Lord is expected to appear. This is based on an old belief that a naming was considered a bringing forth. It could be considered the manifestation of Christ, and it happened at the culmination of the Mass.

Jung said that this ritual act is not a human action but a divine event. He notes that the Mass tries to include the believer in the process of transformation; and the believer is represented as a sacrificial gift along with Christ. It is my understanding from reading Jung that the Mass tries to identify the priest and congregation with Christ through the participation in the Mystery where the soul is taken into Christ and contrastingly, Christ is also remembered in the soul. In this way, both God and the individual are transformed. Christ, God, has become literally present in the Euchrist, and each individual will receive Him and be changed. Jung believes that this implies the Mass is a replication of the Incarnation. Jung states that in order to have an awareness of the transformation process rites and dogmas must be experienced as inner events. We cannot experience them as something outside of us. He suggests that being able to follow the meaning of the ceremony would be psychologically and powerfully effective.

Jung relates the symbolic relevance of the Mass to the "individuation process": the integration and wholeness of the human being.

> *Symbols are not allegories and not signs: they are images of contents which, for the most part, transcend consciousness. We have still to discover that such contents are*

> *real, that they are agents with which it is not only possible but absolutely necessary for us to come to terms.*
> *(C.G. Jung, Vol.5, CW, parg. 114, p.77–78)*

Psychologically, Christ, the Son of Man, represents a wholeness that includes and goes beyond the ordinary man. Jung suggests this notion corresponds to our total personality, our Self, which is beyond our full awareness. Jung makes the case that the mystery of the Eucharist, which is symbolically expressed by Christ, transforms our souls and brings us into our wholeness. In this sense, he regards the Mass as the *rite of the individuation process.* (C.G. Jung, CW, Vol.11, Parg. 414, p.273.). Just as rites and dogmas must be experienced as inner events, so, too, one can only be aware of this transformative process of individuation by experiencing it inwardly. Individuation is a very painful process involving suffering. There needs to be an awareness of the transformative process so it is experienced as a change within one's own psyche (soul). Jung says that if we stop our projections and no longer identify ourselves with others' opinions then the Self (our total personality) will work to unify the opposites within us, creating a harmony and balance. From the perspective of psychology, Jung believes this process forms the most immediate experience of the Divine that can be imagined. (C.G. Jung; CW, Vol. 11; Psychology and Religion).

Many years ago my dad told me a story about a very hot Sunday morning when his mother was walking with him to church. In fact, it was Saint Martin's Church. One-way, it was a walk of nearly ten kilometers. He was about age seven. Perhaps it was around the time he would be making his first communion. He recalled how terribly hot it was and how thirsty they were on the walk. He said, "Mother reached into her purse, and pulled out a stick of gum. She tore it in two and gave me half." As he shared this memory, he had a happy smile on his face. His eyes grew wet. He looked away. Was there anymore that needed to be said? We both knew that fasting was a requirement. No one could receive communion, the Body of Christ, if they had eaten, or chewed gum. It would be a breach. Yet, the sharing of chewing gum on that hot morning may well have been a true giving and receiving of the Living Water (the presence of God's grace). An inner knowing of the right thing to do without the input of external opinions. Would Jesus, who offered Living Water to the Samaritan woman at the well, not approve? Surely, if we summon him, the God who lives in all of us will guide us.

Dad's story was unlike one I had been told years later by an older businessman I knew. This man was in his seventies at the time, and his story illustrated a situation where the self is unconscious. He told me that when he was about seventeen, he was visiting with his grandparents one weekend. On Sunday morning his grandfather had to go to town. His grandmother told him to return by suppertime because she wanted to go to the evening Service at their church. During that winter afternoon a blizzard arose. As the storm worsened, grandmother seemed to grow more worried and restless. Suppertime arrived and grandfather still wasn't home. It was just past six thirty when the team of horses hauling the sleigh with grandfather came into the yard. Grandfather took the horses into the barn and then came into the house. Grandmother was not only annoyed that he was late for supper, but that he had put the horses in the barn when she needed to take them with the sleigh to get to Church. Grandfather said to her, "You can't take those horses out again tonight. They're exhausted coming through that blizzard!"

Grandmother exclaimed, "I don't care! I'm taking them and going to Church, just the same!"

Grandfather looked at her and quietly said, "Yes. And you'll come back, just the same."

Let us remember, "Only what's done for Christ will last." In this very brief time we call life, perhaps the most important and lasting thing we can do is to seek and follow the divine within us. We can always find Christ within, if we seek Him there; for that is where our divinity is hidden.

The Post Office

My older sister, Rita, said she remembered the day I was born. I looked at her waiting to hear what, in particular, she remembered. My stare prompted her to continue. She said, "I remember it because that morning Mama wrote a letter to the doctor, and I had to run it over to the Post Office before the mail truck came." A silly sense of excitement came over me when she said that. It was the thrill of knowing that the Post Office had been a part of my life even on my journey here. I felt like the last piece of the puzzle had been snapped into place in my understanding of the fondness and pleasure of my Post Office memories. The announcement of my impending arrival was carried through the Post Office.

The fascination and reality of those times had an appeal that by today's ways and means makes the facts seem magical or, at least, unbelievable. Reaching the doctor by mail to attend a birth, on the same day as you wrote the letter, is mind-boggling considering that sometimes you can't reach them today with a phone call and expect a response within the week. The midwife, Nancy, could be summoned more informally and more rapidly as she lived only a few houses beyond the Post Office and within a few minutes running distance. She had already been there to assist Mother with her previous twelve deliveries. Each one as surely, safely and lovingly delivered as the mail. I would make *the baker's dozen.*

The Post Office was a place of mystique for me. In fact, my happiest childhood memories are linked to the Post Office and the henhouse. When my siblings didn't want to go get the mail or gather the eggs, I was always a willing volunteer, until it seemed these became my official tasks. When I heard my sisters complain about having to do the dishes or sweep the floor, or my brothers grumble about having to cut kindling or carry firewood into the house, I'd think, I must have the best jobs because I loved getting the mail and gathering eggs. Once, in a moment of gigantic generosity, when my brother was making a fuss about having to carry in some firewood, I offered that he could go get the mail and I would carry in the wood. He didn't take me up on the offer. The woodshed was not nearly as far to go as the Post Office. It didn't bother me in the least. I had helped out with doing dishes and carrying wood before, and I knew those jobs had no real thrill or excitement to them.

While all household chores carried a sense of importance and responsibility for growing children, there was no magic in many of them. Unless you made it for yourself. Of course, we were expected to be careful and not break dishes. Of course, care had to be taken with handling an axe when chopping wood. Accidents sometimes happened. But we were taught how by example, then trusted and expected to do the job right. Each task had its own level of responsibility and importance in the overall flow of life. There were enough of us that no one would get away with half measures. Either someone would blab on you, or they would help you out to make sure things got done right.

My self-assigned jobs also held important responsibilities. The eggs had to be carefully handled and brought to the house without breakage. In the morning, the hens heard you coming, and they were ready to be released into the fresh air and brightness of the day. You made sure, as you turned that latch, to stand behind the door as you opened it because the hens were both running and flying out of there at the same time. You didn't want to be in their way. They'd show no mercy. Yet, that dangerous thrill was always followed by your pupils adjusting to the darkness of their space and the warmth on the eggshells as you gathered the morning eggs. The final gathering of the day included making sure all the hens were back inside the henhouse for the night and the door was closed and securely latched. You were not to make it easy for the foxes. It was similar to mailing a letter or bringing home the mail; a carefulness and vigilance was brought to the task. No piece of mail was to be grabbed and captured by the wind. A protective bag or covering must accompany you in rain or sleet. There was, after all, paper with ink words formed on it that someone needed to be able to read.

The big difference for me, between gathering eggs and gathering mail, was in the speed of my return carrying the cargo. I held on to the mail tightly and sometimes it was safely zipped inside my jacket. If I tripped or fell, it likely wasn't going to break. Eggs, however, had to be transported with the same surety with which the hen fulfilled its purpose daily. It was not an act to be followed up by the carelessness of an unappreciative child. The hen's purpose meant a breakfast or, perhaps, a chocolate cake. Getting those eggs to the house uncracked was as important as ensuring the mail reached its destination safely and on time.

The earliest memory of my going to the Post Office was with an older sibling. I was about four or five and she was about twelve. Aside from the likelihood that I served the function of mail carrier in training, I would soon be starting school and had to learn about the larger world beyond my yard and my grandfather's yard next door. I would have to cross the road both to attend school and to get to the Post Office. The General Store, which I would eventually go to, but rarely ever on my own, was also on the opposite side of the road from my home. Even the garden growing the vegetables to feed our family was positioned across the road and near the ocean access. One might wonder how we kept animals out of our garden as it was out of view. That wasn't so much of a problem as wild animals had their own homes that were not overtaken and destroyed by humans in those times. However, if a rabbit, such as Peter, was to investigate the garden, we would probably have been enjoying our vegetables in a rabbit stew a few evenings later. It was how life rolled. But I digress. As I think of it now, I may have grown up on the wrong side of the tracks. Nevertheless, knowing how to safely cross the road and check for any oncoming cars or trucks was vital.

Each time I accompanied someone to the Post Office, I was inevitably the shortest and youngest hopeful in the usually crowded entry. From my low vantage point I could survey the boots on the ground all the way up the array of garments to the hats on the unfamiliar heads. I came to learn who these people in the community were in this place of business and social interaction. The names I heard spoken I assigned to the appropriate faces. Sometimes the faces were god-offal, and I would have to study them for a bit to convince myself they were real and not Hallowe'en masks. It was then I would feel the hard elbow nudge followed by the whisper, "Don't stare," from my sister, Brenda. All of the people getting mail seemed older than anyone I knew except for my grandfather. They weren't though. They just dressed in dark and dreary clothes and some didn't smile. At times I would slightly cower behind my sibling as if to be protected from their frowns. Sometimes, there were older men who seemed to smile too sweetly at me and evoked the same frightened response. There were also the pleasant, lovely people who smiled and acknowledged everyone present and generally had something cheerful to say. I recall asking my sister on our way back home one day about an old person who wore boots, dark leggings, a long skirt with a shorter, long overcoat on top. Her hair was pulled tightly back and covered with a hair net, with a round, pill-box type, hat on her head. Her hands looked like they belonged to a man. She seemed to wear a perpetual frown and never spoke to anyone. When I asked my sister why that person looked so grumpy, I was told to not worry about her, she probably just had a bee in her bonnet. At the time, the explanation was sufficient.

In the late fifties people, in my locale, wore clothing made mostly from wool or cotton, and the garments made from these fabrics were worn until they were worn out or out-grown. It seemed in our family, and in our community, there was no frivolous buying of garments. You got them because you needed them. Of course, there were silks and satins, but those were worn for occasions like weddings and Christmas. They were not Post Office attire. A bag of hand-me-downs was received with the same reverence and gratitude as a gift from the gods. No doubt, it was. Yet, those weren't the packages arriving through the Post Office; and they never embodied the depth of mystery or anticipation as mailed parcels. Packages arriving through the Post Office were, generally, from mail order catalogues, and, most often, required a payment of cash on delivery. These COD's meant another degree of importance and responsibility for the Postmistress and her Office. The Post Office in Spry Harbor, or, to me, Eileen's Post Office, was the first to be assigned the credential of processing money orders. This meant that you could pay for your mail orders when you placed them by giving the Postmistress your money, and she would give you a money order that could only be redeemed by the recipient. It was stamped showing it came from the Post Office and you had to sign it. You could also send money safely to other people and only they could get the cash by taking their money order to another authorized Post Office or a bank. Cash could be removed by any light fingers; but a money order would have to be forged. A Federal offence. Our modern-day e-commerce had its beginnings at the post office.

Both the darkness of the brown varnished or painted lathed walls, and the closed door leading into the place where the Post Mistress carried out her duties added to the sense of suspense that hung in that entry. We were served through an opening in the wall which had a shelf like a window ledge. People could set their gloves and mail there. It could be closed off completely by sliding a matching dark brown board across the only access to our precious mail. The darkness of the place was not so much scary as it was mysterious. After all, there was a window on the right of the entry that allowed daylight inside. But the space was just dark enough to hold the wonderment of the place with all those sealed letters and wrapped parcels. A child could only imagine what was inside.

The Postmistress was Eileen Bollong, a woman I grew to love. She was consistent, reliable and trustworthy. She gave good advice like "tie that scarf back around your neck before you go outside," or "that's going to need another stamp." She knew her business. I admired that. She went about her work with the confidence, organization and efficiency that I had witnessed in my own mother, working around the house. Neither of them missed a beat in the thoroughness of their work while they also attended to the needs of those around them. Maybe that's why I loved her so; and, besides, she looked after the Post Office.

Once, when I went late in the afternoon to pick up a parcel, the dark gray, heavy canvas mailbag sat in the entry all secured and ready to be picked up by the mail truck driver. I could smell it. I breathed that stinky smell in deeply as if to savor every letter inside. To this day, I don't smell canvas without a happy thought of that mailbag. As Eileen was getting my parcel, a man hurried through the door wanting to know if his letter could still make the day's mail. It was very close to closing time, and Eileen probably hoped she was done with the public for the day when she secured that mailbag for pick up. Nevertheless, glances were made toward the mailbag, and Eileen hid any annoyance well. She said, "Well, you just made it in time. I'll get it in there for you." I was handed my parcel, and the man followed me out the door, happy and still expressing thanks to Eileen.

The only person I knew who lived in the community, but I had never seen at the Post Office was Loretta. I saw her almost every morning, but never at the Post Office. Another mystery for a little mind to figure out. Loretta's job was to keep the children warm. She had snow-white hair and walked rather awkwardly and somewhat stooped. I had been told that she walked that way because she was bow-legged. It looked painful to me, but she didn't seem to mind or ever appear cranky about it. Every school day from late summer through late spring, and in all kinds of horrible weather, Loretta walked from her home to our one-room schoolhouse and made the morning fire. It was made in a fifty-gallon oil barrel that was centrally located, in the classroom, and served the purpose of heating our learning space. From the front window of our home, we could witness her arrival at the school across the road. On the stormiest of winter mornings, when we hoped, we didn't have to get out of our pajamas, we would see Loretta, and we knew we were going to school. I only remember one blustery morning when Loretta had not shown up yet and it was 8:15 a.m. That day, there was no school. I think I was about age seven when I figured it out that Loretta must have stopped to get the mail on her way home from making the fire. After all, the mail truck would have gone through by then, and her mail would be ready for pick up. I assume that is why I never got to see her at the Post Office.

At times the mail was heavy for a smaller child to carry, like on those days, a few times a year, when the Eaton's and Simpson Sears catalogues arrived. There would be a lot of shifting the load from arm to arm on the walk home. The weight was there but so was the lightness of the joy I knew I carried. I knew how much pleasure those catalogues held, and I felt like I was bringing home a treasure for the whole family to enjoy.

Occasionally a parcel would arrive, usually around Christmastime, fulfilling orders placed from those catalogues. A couple of times Eileen told me that one of the older kids had to come pick up the parcel because it was too big, or difficult, for me to carry home. She had the skill of being able to assess the capacity of the carrier. This was important as it ensured that the goods passing through her Post Office reached their destination safely. Another requirement of the Postmistress was her ability to discern who was to receive the ambiguous mail. For instance, when a letter came addressed "To The Folks Down Home". How was that to be sorted? She not only had to know, and probably did, but she also had to remember who had left the community, traveled away and would be corresponding so casually and familiarly to those left behind. It was only after this exercise of the mind that she could ensure appropriate delivery. Today there would be no hope of that letter reaching its intended recipient.

By the time I was old enough to go to the Post Office by myself, about age seven, I was also tall enough to see through the service window. There was another door inside the Post Office that led to the kitchen of Eileen's home. Sometimes the door would be left open a bit. Full of curiosity, I would try my best to peer into the house, and imagine how special it must be to live there in a place actually attached to the Post Office. Eileen, without turning her head from her work, seemed to be aware of my gawking, and with nothing but the movement and sweep of her arm behind her, she would slam that door shut.

Things did happen behind that door. Not just the ordinary things of family life which were probably much like my own experiences; but I felt important Post Office business must extend into that space. Sure enough. One day I was to learn that I had not just imagined things.

During the celebratory seasons when the mail was abundant and difficult to process without mechanization, more magic took place behind the Post Office door and at the family's kitchen table. Christmas and Easter were times of reaching out with greetings and well wishes; reminders to family, friends, business associates and fond acquaintances that they were thought of and remembered by others. The manifestation of love and good will carried through the Post Office. Everyone sent and received greeting cards during these occasions. This volume of cards and their timely delivery was surely a heavy burden to an already busy, daily workload. But it had to be done. The Royal Mail must go through! That was an unquestionable concept in rural Canada.

During these busier times, Eileen's older children were assigned the important responsibility of ensuring a one cent, and later, a two-cent stamp, which had been purchased through the Post Office, was secured to each envelope. Then the inked stamp had to be placed on top of it showing its official status and importance. It also signified the fact that it had been processed by the Post Office and would be formally delivered to the addressee. People could and would drop their letters and cards, along with their pennies for postage, in the mail slot outside the Post Office door. Eileen would unlock the box inside and remove the mail and the money for the stamps which she or her children would ensure got on the envelopes. A couple of teenage siblings would not miss the opportunity to insert their own fun into a monotonous task that did not seem magical to them, but had to be done at their mother's request. The unexpected and frequent stamping on your sister's or brother's arm would prove beneficial. It certainly added excitement, anger, laughter, and perhaps, parental intervention, to an otherwise humdrum job. For myself, I may have imagined scribbling an address on the arm before stamping it, and having a sibling shipped off to parts unknown.

Although I didn't ship any siblings off anywhere, when I was nine years old, I did employ the postal services for my first personal purchase, other than candy. In the cupboard that held some canned goods reserved for our lunches, I spotted a promotion on the Campbell's tomato soup can. It said I could mail away twenty-five cents along with labels from two Campbell's soup cans to the address given, and they would send me the Campbell's soup doll. She was a soft rubber doll about eight inches tall and wore a sweet smile. She also wore a chef's white hat over her painted yellow hair, and a white dress with a red aproned skirt. She even wore white socks and shoes. My desire to have her had nothing to do with how she looked. I knew they would send her to me through the Post Office. I could hardly wait. I removed the labels from two cans and held onto them until I could earn and save up the required twenty-five cents I needed to make the purchase. When the big day arrived, my sister gave me a five-cent stamp and an envelope which I prepared with the address from the label. I checked. It was the same address on both labels. I inserted those labels and sealed the envelope. Oops! I forgot to put the quarter inside. Panic surged through my body. It was my first major mail order, and I had carelessly botched things up. My sister, who from that moment on I admired for her brilliance, suggested we could steam the envelope open and insert the quarter. The tea kettle was boiled and the steam directed over the sealed envelope to moisten and soften the glue. This was definitely an art. I don't know where she learned it. When the quarter was dropped inside, the envelope resealed, and some scotch tape applied as an extra security measure, I ran to the Post Office with my letter. Just as they promised, I had my doll in about three weeks. She was everything I expected. But the biggest thrill was the day she arrived and I picked her up at the Post Office. She never gave me as much joy or pleasure since.

As Postmistress, Eileen had personal contact with someone from every household in the community, if not on a daily basis, at least, weekly. The one person she was sure to see twice daily was the driver of the mail truck, Harry Henley. He was as reliable and vigilant in his duties as Eileen. The severity of the weather didn't seem to matter. In blizzards or heavy rains the mail truck went by our house five mornings a week, except for holidays, even if the weather delayed its arrival by a couple of hours later than usual. The cold and snow drifts may have prevented me and my little legs from trudging to the Post Office, but it didn't seem to stop Harry and the mail truck. His cargo would be safely delivered, and Eileen would be waiting. There was an expression, or belief back in those times that the first person, of the opposite sex, you saw on February fourteenth, Valentine's day, was your Valentine. Eileen had the fated surety that Harry, the mail truck driver, was likely going to be her Valentine. And a sweetheart he was, for he also brought Valentine greeting cards to many of us from friends and family everywhere.

Today's technology allows us to say or write just about anything we want and "post it" online. There it is, viral and released for the world to see, if someone chooses to take that message and send it around. The only magic or mystery in that, it seems to me, is that I have no idea how it happened. There is no privacy in the message. It is not hidden from everyone's view in an envelope or package; and no one has to go to the trouble of even steaming it open or resealing it. No matter what the message is, it has the casual, rushed and unimportant greeting of a postcard. Not so important, or personal, if you don't mind everybody reading it. It seems to lack the respect, integrity and care once provided to the sender and recipient of their personal messages through the Post Office. Personal boundaries were not crossed unless some particular scoundrel, maybe a family member, wanted to steam open a letter not addressed to them. That would be frowned upon. Maybe the woman with the man's hands at the Post Office was the archetypal frowner of such indiscreet behaviors. Where is she now when we need her?

In my final days on earth, I may be visiting or traveling abroad, when I will unexpectedly depart this life. I can only hope that I will be cremated and shipped home through the Post Office to my final resting place. Beginning and ending my journey here through the Post Office! I can't imagine a happier culmination. Perhaps someone will receive me with the same thrill and anticipation I once experienced receiving a Campbell's soup doll.

Just So You Know

As I sat on the sofa working a Sudoku puzzle, Doug sat in his chair, as if watching TV, but with the sound muted. He suddenly and unexpectedly turned toward me and said, "You know that guy you used to like?"

I looked at him shocked. As our eyes met, I saw that he knew I would know. I simply said, "What about him?"

Doug answered, "Well, he lied to you!" He turned his head away back toward the television, but his eyes shifted back toward me. He added, "Just so you know!" Then he looked away.

This subject had not been mentioned in over thirty years, and even back then, it was always him raising the memory of Barry, a past boyfriend. Each time it had been with sudden onset and began with, "Remember that guy?" or "You know that guy?"

Every time I would anger and say, "I am not discussing him with you."

But he always completed it with, "He lied to you."

I stared at him in disbelief for what seemed a long time. I wondered what had stirred that memory. Why would I need to know that, and why would either of us even care? I hadn't seen that guy in nearly fifty years. As my husband's health continued to decline, I had noticed that his thoughts often took him to old memories and to worries about me and my well-being should he someday not be there with me. A feeling of love and compassion filled me, and I got up and stood behind his chair, leaned over and kissed his forehead. Doug leaned his head back to kiss me on my lips. I asked if he'd like a cup of tea. He said, "If you're having one." I went into the kitchen to prepare the tea and in a few minutes, I heard him shout, "Bourdain's on!" We both enjoyed that program, and Anthony Bourdain, in particular. We sat, with our tea, and watched it together. In the weeks and months to follow, I never thought of that moment again. As strange as it seemed, it felt equally unimportant.

Just two nights earlier we had shared a beautiful Valentine's evening together at our favorite Italian restaurant. It was very special and memorable. We thoroughly enjoyed it. We, like all the other lovers dining there that evening, were treated like royalty. I had no way of knowing that in just three weeks he would be gone.

The thoughtfulness and generosity of people during these past few months has been such a blessing to me; especially the kindness and attention of my sons and their wives; it's as if they can't do enough for me. But I wonder, how long can this last? Perhaps that is just how thoughts float in the midst of loss because you don't know what changes tomorrow may bring.

At the funeral, a friend, who had previously lost her son, and was intimate with grief, told me to accept every invitation that comes along. She said it would help me to deal with my sorrow if I stayed engaged with people. For the most part, I've been doing that; still I go to bed alone, wake up alone, have my coffee alone without him to discuss plans for the day, or share a laugh about our night time dreams. And his chair remains empty.

The invitation from my son, on this Saturday afternoon, is to come for a lobster cookout tomorrow at his place. I am delighted and reply that I would love to go, although I had made tentative plans for Sunday. The invoice for the headstone arrived yesterday. I thought I would drive the two hours to the cemetery tomorrow to see if the monument was what I had ordered before I paid the bill. One more task completed in closing out a life. I may have to put the trip off until Wednesday depending on the time lobsters are being served. If it's midday I won't try to rush down and back tomorrow. When you are adrift in life your time doesn't seem important. Days all run together. It is ten-thirty Sunday morning when I receive a text saying, "We will eat at five o'clock; but come anytime." I don't reply. I decide I have time to get ready, make the return trip and pay a quick visit to my oldest sister who hasn't been feeling well.

She had called on Thursday night to check on me. Being a widow, herself, she knew about long evenings. When I told her I was making cabbage rolls, she said she wished she had some. I remember to take the container of left-over cabbage rolls out of the fridge to give to her.

I stayed with her longer than I had planned, but we enjoyed a good visit. Then, I continue on my way. It is about two-thirty when I turn off the highway toward the cemetery. I am surprised to see dozens of cars parked outside the church. The door to the church is open. It doesn't look like it is a funeral or a wedding, and I know it can't be a typical Sunday service as there aren't that many people who live in the community if you combine all denominations. I meander toward the cemetery road and park my vehicle on the roadway near my husband's grave.

As I walk toward the burial site, the new polished black stone, with its inlaid grey pillars, stands out among the other more weathered stones nearby. I know he would be pleased with it. I am, too, for it is stately and dignified befitting the man whose resting place it marks. Our oldest son who helped me choose this stone would like to see it and, since he resides at the other end of the country, I take a few photos with my phone to forward to him. As I stand there reading the engraving it occurs to me that this is not "his" stone, but "our" stone for my name and birthdate are also engraved there looking like some unfinished business to be completed at another time. It was against the wishes of all three boys that I had my name put on the stone, but it made more financial sense to have it engraved now. One of them said he didn't want to visit his father's grave and see my name there, too. I suppose that would stir the orphan within whose time had not yet come. I mused that at least I didn't share the fate of John Irving's character, Owen Meaney, and arrive to see my termination date included.

The sound of a vehicle on the gravel road brings me back to the moment. I look and see that it has stopped at the bottom of the roadway that cuts through the middle of the cemetery, designed for the convenience of the hearse, but where I have conveniently parked today. "Damn," I whisper aloud to no one. "Why is it every time I come here someone else needs to be visiting the graveyard?" I assume the driver wants to bring his car up the driveway and sees I am blocking the road. I say a quick goodbye to my dead husband and start toward my vehicle to move it out of the way and to head back to the city.

I click my key to unlock my truck and smile to myself at the mindlessness of habits. Surely it never entered my mind that some rogue soul would emerge from a grave, jerry-rig my truck and make off with it while I stood there twelve meters away. Yet, I take safety precautions. As I fasten my seatbelt, I glance in the rearview mirror and proclaim another "Damn" as the intruding car has continued along the road and will now meet me as I exit. I pause and decide I am not backing down this hill. I know this road well and the only place wide enough for two vehicles to pass by each other is immediately ahead of me. As I edge forward and pull over toward the right the oncoming car approaches and pulls toward the left.

A cousin, Steve, jumps out of the car and hurries toward my vehicle. I am so focused on him and his urgent approach, I don't notice anyone else in his car. I put down my window and say hello, and in his quickening pace he is saying, "You know how we are cousins; well, I have cousins on the other side of my family too…" but before he finished, I knew.

I whisper, "Barry," and glance toward his car. Somehow I knew. Coming around the front of the car was my cousin's wife, Holly, and Barry.

The moment he caught my glance he smiled and yelled, "Hi, Dyan."

I returned his smile and said, "Hi Barry."

I nodded a hello to Holly which I can only attribute to the impulse of inbred good manners, as I felt totally accosted and overwhelmed with what was happening. Amidst my ego voice challenging the pounding of my heart, and somewhere in the ethers hearing my husband's voice asking, "What's going on?"

I managed to calmly ask, in what certainly could have been an Oscar winning performance, "What brings you here, Barry?"

An image of Salvador Dali's *Collapse of Time* found its way into the rush of recall while I experienced a synergy of what time had done, and left undone. Suddenly, another flashback and my husband's voice saying, "He lied to you. Just so you know." My head was spinning, and I was fighting for my composure with all I had. I heard a voice inside my head say, *You don't know him; if you passed him on the street, you wouldn't even know him...* Another voice, that seemed to come from my heart, interrupted with, *Shut Up!* This was a command I never spoke nor would I allow my children to say those words because everyone has a right to speak and be heard. Yet, here it was coming from within and intending to be noticed.

Fortunately, I didn't faint as one might expect from the whirling dizziness passing through me. A strange calm came over me. I felt I was presenting cool and contained, but I dared not remove my sunglasses as my eyes would betray me. I knew I couldn't get out of the truck because I had never practiced standing or walking on rubber legs, and this didn't seem the right moment for such an experiment. Instead, I let my elbow rest on the window opening and held my right hand on the steering wheel with the engine running as if, at any moment, I was about to "give er" and show them what I had under the hood of my thirteen-year-old truck. Hoping against all odds that the inner turmoil, memories, emotional eruptions, and my husband's words would not interrupt the clarity of the external sensory information from these special moments I had just been given. Every word, every observation and sensation was being imprinted and would be added to the archive of our time together. I would not miss any of it. My brain had never worked so hard.

From the responses that followed I realized my question seemed ambiguous. Barry replied that he had come for a feed of lobster, and I answered in my forced, swaggering casualness, "Well it's the right time of the year for it." Steve seemed to have interpreted my question as, "what brings you to the cemetery," and he began an explanation of this fortuitous and inexplicable reunion with his own question.

"Do you know what's going on at the Church today, Dyan?"

I replied with what could have been a response to the whole situation, "I have no clue what's going on."

He continued. "It's the Community Men's Choir doing their year end performance. He added that he had been asked to join the group but refused as he felt he couldn't sing. Today he decided to take a drive and stop by the church, and that he had just parked his car when I drove by. He said when he saw me, he told the others, "Oh, there goes Dyan now!" Apparently, Barry had been asking about me just moments before my appearance. While Steve and I spoke, I noticed Barry had walked off to our left and was fixing his shirt inside his pants; adjusting his look.

Steve was telling me that Barry leaned forward from the back seat and asked in surprise, "Dyan Hunter?"

When my identity was confirmed and my married name, Dyan Wilson, up-dated for him, Barry replied, "Oh, I've got to see her!" The decision was made to follow me to the cemetery. It appears I was approached with caution; perhaps to not disturb my visit there, or maybe to observe me from a distance before advancing for a closer look.

After our initial greetings Barry approached my truck and then retreated. At first, I asked myself, would I know him if we passed on the street? There was a sadness on his face that seemed to weigh him down and age him. Other than that, he looked like the years had been good to him. I wondered if he would have recognized me or if he would even give me a second glance. Probably not, as my hair was dark when he knew me and not this lightened color to hide the gray and feign youthfulness.

He stood about three meters away, turned and looked at me and said, "You were such a big part of my life back then. We used to correspond; for a few years, I think. You were a big part of my life!" I observed that the more he thought of "us" the more restless he became and the more he paced toward and away from the truck. Each time he approached me and spoke, he took his sunglasses off. I knew he wanted me to remove mine so he could look into my eyes. I knew that strategy, but I was not about to cooperate. They were the only shield I had. An intimacy and vulnerability had rolled in like a fog surrounding me. He walked away and stared at the ground. Then he came toward me again, saying in a dismissive tone, meant to minimize the emotions that had been stirred, "God, we were just kids."

He addressed me, "What were you, twelve or something?"

I smiled and answered, "I think you were sixteen."

He said, "I think we met at a ballpark or something." I lost contact with his remaining words as I thought to myself, *You know exactly where and how we met, and why you came climbing into the bleachers to sit beside me.* As I tuned in again to his words, he seemed to be wondering aloud what happened to us, and as he approached the truck he hesitantly said, "I think there was a boyfriend…" and left his statement hanging. I felt an annoyance surge through me with how he pretended to struggle with his memories but, in fact, he remembered everything, even more truth than he spoke. I didn't take my eyes off him.

I simply responded by pointing my thumb backward toward my husband's grave and said, "He was the boyfriend!"

Simultaneously, I heard two voices, Steve's saying, "Doug was her boyfriend," and Barry's voice saying, "I suppose you had a lot of boyfriends!" It was Barry's voice I turned to with a look of disgust, and saw in his face the guilt in his projection.

I turned away and said, "Yeah, where is that list of all my boyfriends, it must be here somewhere." I saw Steve smiling, engrossed in the performance before him. He knew I had been with my husband, as girlfriend and wife, for fifty years. A fulfilling life not requiring boyfriends.

There was some intermittent chatter about swatting flies. The tone shifted and Barry asked where I was living now. I answered that I live in an apartment in the city. He asked if I had ever been to Alberta and began to speak of the little hamlet where he lives.

I watched him intently as he spoke about his life. His singularity stood out. He spoke about his home, his backyard, his community, and how he relaxed. I noticed there was no mention of we, us or our; only, I and my. I couldn't imagine he was single, and I wondered if he was divorced or widowed. There was no indication that he had a partner in life. If he did, there was a striking difference to the way he spoke compared to my husband. I knew my husband would have spoken in terms of we and ours. He always did. I found myself searching Barry's hands for a wedding band. There was none. I know many men don't wear wedding bands, and many men travel without their wives even on a holiday. I heard him tell Steve that he relaxed; "sitting by my fire pit in my backyard"; then, smiling, he added, "There's plenty of whiskey in the cupboard." As I watched, I felt a deep sadness for him. During this time, there was no pacing, just standing still and sharing information.

Suddenly Barry turned and walked farther away holding his sunglasses in his hand. I could not take my eyes off him. I saw him turn sideways and stare at the ground a few feet in front of him. He seemed to be deep in thought. Before my eyes, I saw a change in his countenance; a look I can only describe as rapture. It was a look that erased years off his face. I had caught a glimpse of a young man I once knew. I remembered how sensitive and private he was. He turned and came toward me again. He was saying, "We had some beautiful days! We had some beautiful days, didn't we?"

I was nodding my head, yes. Then, standing before me, he looked directly into my shielded eyes repeating, "We had some beautiful days, didn't we! Didn't we!"

I said, "Yes. We did. Yes, we did." He covered his eyes with his sunglasses and left them on. I still would not remove mine because I knew my eyes would show what my heart was feeling. I was vigilant to ensure my eyes and my lips revealed no emotions.

Not once did he acknowledge my reason for being at the cemetery nor did he ever express any sympathy for my loss. I didn't want to ask about a wife, but I did ask about his parents. I said, "Barry?" He turned and looked at me surprised, for I had not spoken much during this encounter. I asked, "Are both your parents still living?" He turned, looked down, made a half-ward body turn before he turned toward me to answer. It was a movement I remembered so well. It was like his signature to me. I had never seen anyone else do that in my life. It was those couple of seconds he would take in deciding how he was going to reply.

When he looked back at me, he said, "My mom is." I waited but he offered nothing more. I knew it meant he didn't want to talk about it.

I commented that I had to get going. Steve came to the truck and said, "I want to give you a hug Dyan." I reached my arms out the window opening, and we embraced.

Holly was right behind him and said, "I have a hug for you, too."

We embraced. As we did, I heard Barry say, "I've got to get me one of them." He put his arms through the window and hugged me. I accepted but did not return his embrace. At that moment I was feeling numb. Maybe I was still fighting my feelings; maybe I felt my husband was watching, or maybe I was still hurting from our breakup. I don't know the reason. Maybe I was afraid I wouldn't let him go.

Casually I said, "It was nice to see you again, Barry." He said, "It was nice seeing you too." We said our goodbyes, and Steve remarked that they were going to take a walk over to Paul's grave before they left. Driving off I see Barry in my rear-view mirror; just standing there with his head hanging, looking at the ground. I could feel the tears beginning to well up in my eyes, like water does before the damn breaks. It was the feeling I had known every summer when he left to return to his home. The tears began to flow freely for a lost love I had never grieved, and for a longing for my true love.

As I make the turn around the top of the cemetery road, I pass by Paul's grave. He had died so young; so tragically in a car accident, only nineteen. I try to remember the last time I saw Paul. I think it had been one summer when he had given Barry a drive to my place in his car. Paul had been a mutual friend to both Barry and Doug, yet the two of them had never met. That brought in the memory of one summer evening. It was in July of that same year. It seemed like a usual Saturday evening when Doug came to see me; but that night there was a joy, a delight in his eyes I had never seen before. There was a lightness to his whole being. It was a striking difference in him. I had to ask, "Why are you so happy tonight?" I recall, the smile never left his face but his eyes gave a flicker.

He sat down and said, "I saw Paul Carty today at the gas station. God it was good to see him! I haven't talked to him in years. We had a great visit today." Bewildered, I asked if he and Paul were friends, as I had never heard him mention his name before. The joyful look never left his face as he assured me that he and Paul were old childhood friends, who used to play hockey together on the ponds. I remember trying to understand his expression. It was like a happy relief at seeing Paul. I studied him, even questioned him, knowing there was something more. He insisted that just seeing this old friend had made him so happy. I was not satisfied, but I couldn't figure out what was missing from his explanation, and he wasn't about to tell me. I had never seen anything or anyone give him that much joy. But I knew I recognized that look: a look of fulfillment; a look of victory. Yes, I had seen that look. It was on the faces of Olympic gold medalists, and lottery winners.

In retrospect, and with tears running down my face, I thought, that was really a terrible summer. It was in August that year Barry and I stopped seeing each other. It was the last time I saw him. Until today. Then, a few weeks later, only days before the change of seasons, we learned of Paul's death. It was a tragedy that brought to neighboring communities that deep sadness that permeates everyone when youth and all its potential is lost. When I got the news, I recall wondering if Doug had heard it yet. There were no cell phones and texts then. I awaited his visit. I would be there to comfort him in person. I thought he might be devastated. When he arrived, he looked sad. But all he said was, "It's a terrible thing. He was a great guy."

I commented, "It's nice that the two of you got to see each other this summer." Nothing more was said about it.

The random flooding of memories could not be stopped any more than this flooding of tears.

Next, that August night wanted to be re-lived; the night Barry and I destroyed everything we had been longing for. The weight of this memory felt like it would crush me. He drove here that summer because he would be staying and attending Dalhousie University in the Fall. His last letter said he would call me when he arrived. It was midafternoon when I got his call and he wanted to see me that same Thursday evening.

When the letter arrived, I told Doug that Barry was on his way and I would be seeing him soon. It seemed he noted my anticipation and was upset. He asked me not to see Barry, even begged me to break up with him. I reminded him that he knew this day was coming. In January, when he presented me with that little Birks blue box holding a cameo ring, and asking me to go steady with him, I realized it was time for me to tell him about Barry. Before that I hadn't seen the need to; didn't really think it was any of his business. He had been visiting with me a few months, but I didn't consider him my boyfriend. I tried to avoid telling him at first. I made various excuses about why I couldn't and wouldn't wear the ring, such as I was too young to be going steady. He didn't care about any of my reasons. He just said he wanted to spend the rest of his life with me. He insisted that I should try the ring on because he wanted to see if it fit me. I thought that was silly since I was giving it back anyway. He removed it from the box and put it on my finger. "Yes," I told him, "It's very pretty, but I'm not going to wear it."

I didn't know what came over him. I wondered if it was because we had not seen each other for three weeks over the Christmas break, and he had really missed seeing me. But a ring? He was getting too serious. I didn't want to hurt his feelings, but I thought it was time to tell him about Barry.

His face showed a lot of interest, but no look of surprise. He listened to me speak as if this was not news to him, but more of a verifying. I had a flashing thought that maybe he knows about Barry, but just as quickly dismissed it as not probable. I told him that Barry and I had been writing to each other during the past four years, and that we spent our time together in the summers when he visited here. I also told him that when Barry returns this summer, I will be seeing him, so "I can't be going steady with you."

The only question I remember him asking me was, "Do you love him?"

I replied, "Yes, I think I do." I handed him back the box with the ring inside. He refused to take it.

He said, "You keep it. It fits you. I don't want it back!" I protested; he insisted. He wouldn't take it from me so I sat it down on the nearby end table, and said to him, "I won't wear it."

He asked, "Would it be alright if I keep coming up to see you?"

I replied, "If you want to."

He wanted to. From January to August, he took his sweetness to new heights: Cards, candies, 45s of songs he knew I liked; gifts; sometimes for occasions and sometimes for no occasion at all. Every minute he could spend with me he did. He made sure he lit up my life. It seemed that time flew by until about June. Then the days seemed to drag, and I found myself wishing them away so that August and Barry would soon arrive.

Doug had graduated from College that Spring and was working in the city. He still returned every weekend to see me. I hadn't received a phone call yet, but I knew Barry would soon be here and I'd be seeing him. I reminded Doug on Saturday evening which turned that visit into one of tension and anxiety. He couldn't stop asking me to not see Barry. I'm sure he summoned all of Paul Simon's "Fifty Ways" and a few of his own. He even suggested that I write Barry a "Dear John" letter and he would personally deliver it to him for me. There was no way he could or would understand my want or need to see Barry. When I tried again to reaffirm my position, and reminded him that he knew this was going to take place, he decided he needed to threaten me. He stated firmly, "If you see him, you will probably never see me again. I might never come back here!" I took note of the "probably" and the "might."

I looked him steadily in the eyes and said, "You suit yourself; but I'm seeing Barry." I was surprised at what I didn't say to him, like, what makes you think I'll want to see you again anyway? But I never even thought to say that to him. Now, I wonder if he was challenging me with a truth only he knew about me: that I would never want to lose him. He begged me so much to break up with Barry, I finally said I would just to get him to stop.

On Sunday afternoon, on his return trip to the city, Doug stopped in to see me again. He needed reassurance. He sat with me and held my hands. He said, "I need you to promise me you will break up with Barry." I didn't have all afternoon for this routine again.

I said, "I promise." It was not good enough.

He said, "NO! I want you to look me in the eyes and say, 'I promise to break up with Barry.' Please say it." I did. It must have been convincing. But I remained silent about the rest of my thought, which was, *Unless Barry changes my mind.*

The tears pour down my face, making it almost too hard to see to drive. My shirt is wet. I guess the memory needed washing away because another was about to replace it. A memory I was resisting, but it emerged.

Barry had parked the car and turned his back to the steering wheel to face me. He smiled at me. I had been wondering how I would approach telling him that I had been seeing Doug. I wanted to get it out of the way. In my lack of wisdom, and to ease into the subject, I began by asking him if he had been seeing or dating anyone. I guessed he hadn't been expecting that question. His face grew serious, and he shook his head, no. I saw in his eyes that wasn't true. I noted it, but I didn't care. Why would I? I had been seeing someone, too. I said, "Well, for about the past ten months I've been seeing a guy." I wasn't expecting his question either.

He asked, "Does that mean you don't want to see me?"

In return, I whispered a lie, "Yes." Barry just turned to start the car.

He didn't say a word. He didn't ask, what about us? He didn't say that I meant anything to him. He made no protest. He didn't insist or even suggest we should give us a chance. Everything I wanted to hear from him; everything that would have made me his, he didn't speak. In that moment I experienced deafening silence.

The car wouldn't start. Just like that the alternator quit. After a few attempts to start the car, Barry walked to the highway to flag down assistance. I sat there alone, feeling stunned by his reaction; wanting so much for us to talk about our feelings for each other. All he did was call my bluff. I hoped there would be no traffic and we would be stuck here; then we would talk. Then I began to wonder if or when I would make it back home that night. As the tension continued to mount in me, I heard a song start running through my head. It was the Everly Brothers singing, *Wake Up Little Susie.* I may have missed the message, but I recalled some of the words; something about my *reputation being shot, and being in deep trouble.* Although I smiled to myself, I wondered what would it matter if I was out all night. I was already on the road to hell for being a liar.

Barry returned. He had flagged down his uncle who drove us back to his grandparents. He borrowed his grandfather's car and drove me home. My recall is that everything felt rote and quiet. It seemed that getting rid of me was the only focus left for the evening. On the drive home, Barry and I did not speak a word to each other. I silently prayed he would pull the car over and tell me how much he loved me. I happened to know a guy who would do that. It was the one and only thing I needed to know; to hear from Barry. When he turned into the driveway, I opened the car door, looked at him and said, "Bye."

He glanced at me and said, "Bye." This wasn't the end of Summer "bye," it was a forever "bye." I couldn't and didn't even shed a tear.

I didn't know that prayers were no longer answered once you turn at that interaction on to the road to hell. I also didn't know that sometimes we need to be thankful for unanswered prayers.

The following evening I was at home. My brothers had already left to go see their girlfriends, and I was just cleaning up the kitchen after our supper. I had no plans. I didn't know if Doug would be stopping in or not, and I really didn't care. As I was about to walk out of the kitchen, I heard a rap at the door and in walked Doug. He didn't speak or take his eyes off me as he shut the door behind him. There was a questioning and a hopefulness in his eyes. I said, "Hi."

He walked up to me and asked, "Did you break up with him?"

Again, I whispered, "Yes." He hugged me.

Then he said, "Let's go sit down. I want you to tell me all about it."

I sat on a chair in the family room and he sat on a footstool in front of me. Then he asked, "Did you kiss him?"

I simply said, "No." He smiled. He knew I wouldn't lie to him. He knew I hated it when people told lies. To me it was such a destructive obstacle that would eventually need to be removed because I believed truth would have to prevail. Again I wipe away tears, and blow my nose. The thought comes to me that maybe I am the liar I most hated all these years. Sobs erupted at the possibility.

Regaining control, my thoughts turn to the memory of that Friday night. I had begun by saying to Doug, "Before I told him about you, I asked if he had been seeing anyone, and he said, 'no—"

Interrupting, Doug shouted, "He lied to you! He lied to you!" I was shocked. What did he know about it; and why did he sound so delighted that I had been lied to?

I asked, "What are you talking about?"

He answered, "He lied to you. I saw him walking on Barrington Street holding a girl's hand."

I screamed, "Have you been spying on him? How would you even know him? You don't know him!" I had lost it! I'm sure he felt like the victor, who could calmly inform me of the truth. He assured me that he was not spying on Barry, but that he had seen him around before and could recognize him, and he just happened to be going downtown to the pool hall when he witnessed Barry walking along the street holding some girl's hand. I shouted, "Who cares? Why shouldn't he see other girls; I was seeing you, remember?!"

He reiterated, "But he lied to you!" He seemed to think I didn't grasp what he was saying to me. I didn't tell him I already knew; and I didn't tell him I had lied to Barry either.

I told him, "If you keep this up, you can turn around and walk back out that door you came through," as I pointed to the kitchen. I continued, "I am not going to sit here and listen to you bad mouth Barry. This conversation is over!"

He reached and held my arm. He said, "Okay. I won't." In a few seconds he changed the subject.

Before Doug left that evening, he asked me if I still had the ring. I just looked at him. What did he think I had done with it? He then asked, "Will you wear it?" I didn't answer. I just hugged him. He left saying, "I'll see you tomorrow night." When he arrived on Saturday evening, I was wearing his ring. It was the ring from a man who loved me, and who was strong enough to show me.

I'd like to say I never looked back, but that's not entirely true. It was several years and three children later. I was home alone one cool, Spring morning. I opened my keepsake box. Barry's letters were on the bottom of it. I took them out and returned the box to the closet. Before I read them again, I made a fire in the fireplace. I was melancholy, but I shed no tears as I read each letter before tossing it into the flames. I intended it to be a ritual of closure; a complete letting go that might even bring me a feeling of relief. The lingering would be gone. All I felt was the warmth from the fire. I had never imagined a resurrection. I had never imagined today.

I wiped my eyes and blew my nose until both were red. I'm thinking I will look like a clown from the circus when I arrive at my son's. I have no recall of the drive itself or any of the familiar villages I know I must have driven through. I arrive at the cookout with red, swollen eyes, looking wretched. I didn't care. I had been visiting the graveyard.

Rewards

It was late July and the first morning all month that wasn't misty and thick with fog. The sun made an appearance. It was the day to get the laundry done and hung out on the clothesline. The phone rang about ten o'clock. My cousin, Lily, wanted me to go out in the boat with her and some other, local cousins. Usually, when she arrived, we were like musketeers, but some changes had occurred during the past year and I had more responsibilities. Every summer Lily and her family spent two weeks at their summer place on White's Hill. The house originally belonged to her great grandparents, and was where her grandfather had grown up. Her father owned it now, and came there with his mother, wife and children every summer. Their primary home was in Hopetown, a town outside Boston. Lily's grandmother was my aunt Victoria, my dad's oldest sister. Lily and I called ourselves second cousins, but Aunt Victoria, setting the record straight, told us we were first cousins once removed. I told Lily I wanted to go boating but first I had to hang out the wash and finish up some housework. I could be ready by eleven thirty. She didn't understand. She started going berserk but soon calmed down. She insisted that she and the guys would walk to my house and we'd walk down to the shore together to go boating for the afternoon. She was a sweet, fun girl who was not concerned about responsibilities. Lily and I enjoyed our teen years differently.

During the past year my brothers, Keith and Stu, and I lived alone at home. We took care of the place; the wood and kindling were split and brought in to keep the fires burning, the ashes were taken out as required, household chores were done, meals were made and eaten, and we kept up our grades at school. No missing the bus either! I was vigilant about making sure things were done, and done thoroughly because I felt the three of us did not want to be separated. For the first few years after our mother's death, a brother and his wife lived with us and then a sister and her husband spent a school year with us. That was the year I was in grade seven. Then, we managed on our own for a couple of years. The older ones in the family had their lives, and none of them wanted to be raising three teenagers. That was our saving grace. At the time we never spoke to each other about it. Separation was a bad idea that should not even be entertained. But I later learned that I was not alone fearing someone might convince Dad that we should not be living there by ourselves, and that we might be split apart to go to live with various older siblings. In my mind, I was determined that no one would have any reason to say we could not stay at home together. I had finished grade eight and turned fourteen that summer.

For three teenagers living alone, we got along very well. That may have been due to a private intent to "stay under the radar." At the beginning of our first year at home alone, my youngest brother was encouraged to go to Alberta to live with an older sister and her husband. He tested the promises of excitement and new experiences in a strange land, and found them wanting. He was homesick. He returned home at Christmastime. It may not have seemed like it to him, but I think my joy equaled his upon his return. My older brother enjoyed playing ball and was often at the ballfield. Sometime later, he acquired a drum set. He would play drums during the summers and in the evenings. He was self-taught and showed me a few techniques, but he mostly played them. I dared to clash those cymbals when he was elsewhere. Later on he was the drummer in a band, and he still plays drums today, every day, but for his self-enjoyment only. He's an excellent drummer! We were also preparing for our Confirmation at that time, but since we had no transportation, the parish priest would bring the three other catechumens to our house one Thursday evening a month for instruction. That was the only time there were loud voices or passionate disagreements in our home. Many of the things we were instructed about, we knew were rubbish. None of us would accept that bullshit, even from a priest. During our unsupervised years together, there were only two incidents that were disturbing. One was the day my younger brother came home and ran up to his bedroom. I didn't know what was going on, but something felt odd. I went upstairs and knocked on his closed door, then entered. He was standing there with a cloth wrapped around his hand and terror on his face. The first story he told me was that he just hurt his fingers. I insisted he show me his hand. I saw the blood on the cloth and was as scared as he was of what we'd see. When I saw the skin off his fingers and hanging flesh, my body made that wretched movement that tells the stomach to settle down. Again I asked, "What happened?" This time he confessed. His friend had some firecrackers, gave him some to hold and lit them. They went off in his hand, and he came running home. I told him I had to clean his fingers and bandage them and it might sting. He was very brave as we set to the task. I was thankful it wasn't worse. It could have been. When the wounds were tended, I gave him a lecture that he was never to touch that stuff again, and if his friends had firecrackers, he would not be allowed to play with them. At the time, it wasn't funny, but it humors me now because I am only eighteen months older than him. I guess maybe he wanted or needed some guidance and clarified boundaries. Maybe he just needed to know someone cared about him when he was hurting. We were both thankful, for more reasons than one, that he wouldn't need a doctor. I checked and cleaned the wounds morning and night for a few days. It was healing. He took care of it himself after that. The other frightening experience was the time lightning hit. It was a stormy night and the loud noise woke us at five in the morning. I was frightened but knew I had to go check things out. I went downstairs. The early daylight of June enabled me to see. As I turned at the bottom of the steps, I noticed a scorched mark on the wall by the telephone. I was too nervous to touch the phone so I made my way to the kitchen. There I saw the electric clock that hung on the wall was stopped. As I continued looking around, everything else seemed fine. On my way back to bed I paused and looked at the phone for a long moment. I decided to pick up the receiver. The line was dead. This matter would have to wait until after school. My older brother, lying awake, heard my footsteps. He asked, "What happened?"

I went to his room and said, "Lightning hit the house or nearby." I told him what I saw and that we should try to get more sleep because the bus would be here at eight, and we had exams to write that day. I couldn't get back to sleep. After school I went next door to my oldest brother's home and told him what happened. I had no phone to call anyone, but he knew what to do to get the phone company to come repair it. He came to the house, checked the fuse box and replaced a fuse. The clock had been burned out and it would be a few months before we got another. The next one had batteries.

Grade eight was an eventful, informative and transitional year for me. It was the year I realized some are hopeful for your success; and some hope you fail. But you must not ever put your life and dreams in the hopes of others. Your focus must be on the hopes and dreams you have for yourself. It is your life to live. You must be alert to the opportunities that present themselves, and choose wisely. It's a lot to learn at a young age, but I am not the only one who has been so blessed to learn these things. It seems almost miraculous how we are rewarded every day, either by learning lessons, by our blessings, or by our blessings in disguise.

Lily, Vince, her cousin, and Gill, our mutual cousin, showed up at the agreed time. Gill, a couple of years older than us, seemed to have unlimited access to Lily's uncle Harry's motor boat. When the weather was clear and the sun showed its face, we were in the boat. We usually didn't go on to the islands but we boated around them. We enjoyed the salt spray on our faces as we whipped through the waves. Sometimes we'd see seals sunbathing on coastal rocks and once we even fished from the boat. It felt like freedom. It was our vacation. We would fly kites up on the hill, hang out at each other's houses in the evenings or have bonfires on the rocks at the beach. There we'd steam the periwinkles we had plucked from the seaweed rocks, then pull out the tasty morsels with toothpicks and eat them. We'd visit with aunts and uncles and giggle about stories we heard or told. We could run and jump from rock to rock along the shoreline until we were tired. Then we'd climb on a big rock where we could sit together and talk. It was a time to forget about what needed to be done and just live in the moment. Sometimes I wondered to myself if anyone knew where I was or what I was doing, or if anyone even cared. I guessed Lily had told her parents that I'd be with her on her adventures. I had no one to tell; maybe my brothers before they went off to be with their friends and play ball. Sometimes my older brother worked at the fish plant. Usually we were all back home for supper. On that particular boating day, when I returned home, I brought the clothes in from the line and, after dinner, spent the evening ironing.

Our dad worked away all week and lived in the woods in a logging camp, or in a boarding house near the mill. He was always home by Saturday evening and would return early Monday morning.

On Saturday evening of that same week, I had just cleaned up the kitchen after dinner when company arrived. It was Lily with her dad, Will and her grandmother, my aunt Victoria. It was very unusual for them to visit us at our home as we normally went to White's Hill to visit with them. Not too long into the visit there was some talk about me and all I did around the house; and how clean and well-kept everything looked. I recall feeling uncomfortable being the topic of conversation. But there was some lightness to it as a story was revealed. The story was that Gill had told his mother I ironed clothes better than she did because I even ironed the pockets on the inside of my brother's pants, and she left his pockets all wrinkled up. I laughed with them but critically wondered how anyone could do that: iron and not smooth out the pockets! Will then made the suggestion that I should go to Florida with him and his family over Christmas. Both Dad and I looked at him surprised. Then he said to Dad, "Would it be alright if Darlene came to spend Christmas with us and then come to Florida with us?"

Dad and I looked at each other equally shocked. Dad said, "Well, I guess it would be alright, if she wants to go." He meant it. Suddenly I felt my heart start to race. All eyes were on me when Will asked me if I'd like to go.

I answered, "I'd love to!" Lily squealed. She jumped up and threw her arms around me and hugged me. When her commotion died down, Will said that once he knew their schedule, he would call me to confirm when I would be able to go and he'd mail me an Air Canada ticket. In my mind, it remained to be seen if this would happen. By age fourteen, I had learned to temper my hopes when I was not the sole decision-maker.

In bed that night I lay in the dark thinking about the day and especially about the things that had transpired during the evening. I allowed myself to feel excited about the offer to go to Florida, but I would not allow it to consume my thoughts. Although the idea was thrilling, it was a matter that was completely out of my control, like so many things in my life had been. I learned to focus on the things I could manage and had some control over and that consisted mostly of myself and my behaviors. Lord knows there were enough things in the day to day to keep my mind occupied. I would be going into grade nine in September, and Christmas seemed a lifetime away.

Before falling asleep, I recalled how grade eight had been a busy but fulfilling year. I was elected class representative for the student council, was on sports teams at school that won intramurals, and was part of a successful and enthusiastic track and field team. It was also a year when our school initiated a citizenship award: one for junior high and one for senior high students. The announcement was made in May and the voting took place mid-June. The awards were presented at graduation. The entire student population, about five hundred of us, got to vote for the student "citizen" of their choice. There was no shortlist of candidates to vote for. Theoretically, there could have been five hundred choices. The criteria for voting was to choose the student you felt was an active participant in school activities, performed well academically, someone respectful and courteous to authority figures and their fellow students, and someone you deemed trustworthy, reliable and accountable. I received the majority of votes in the Junior High category. Not only was I completely surprised by that; I was deeply honored. Who wouldn't be? Just to know other students saw you in that light. It wasn't the trophy or the recognition that mattered. I had been shown their regard for me. I will forever be grateful for their respect and encouragement. Just as in any group of children, adolescents or adults, there were those who wanted a different outcome. It was loudly whispered about the corridors that a grade nine student should have won. I ignored it. But it must have seemed that I didn't hear the message because a student came up to me to tell me what was being said. I simply replied, "That's silly. If a grade nine student was supposed to win it then it would only have been open to grade nine students, not all Junior High students." I was never the best or the worst at anything I ever did. But I gave my heart and soul to everything I did. I fell asleep thinking; being fully involved with life makes living good.

In those days, we wrote our exams before our Christmas break from school. December that year became a busy month. I had just received my exam schedule when I got the call from Will. My last exam was on Wednesday, December 21st. He booked my flight for December 22nd and my return flight for January 4th. He mailed the tickets to me; just like he said he would! Now, I knew it was real. I had to plan and organize my life to the minute in those early weeks of December. I knew what I had to study and when; I knew the daily routines that had to be followed; I knew I could be packed with a week of winter and a week of summer clothes by the 20th; and I knew I could get some Christmas baking done between the 20th and the 22nd. I had to, and I did, find a drive home from school on the 21st after I finished my morning exam. I had no time to wait for the afternoon bus.

We were a family that honored tradition. Things were done in the same way year after year. Our Christmas tree was not brought into the house to be decorated until

Christmas Eve. As little children, it was especially delightful to be put to bed on Christmas Eve and to awaken very early to find Santa had been there and the bare evergreen was now sparkling with lights and ornaments and surrounded with beautifully wrapped gifts sprawling out, from underneath it, into the living room. Of course, the largest wool socks we could find were hung with a nail before bedtime and would be bursting with fruit, nuts, candy and a small gift or two by morning. I always thought Santa did it all until it came time that I realized I had to do it myself. The first Christmas we were without our mother, it seemed that the magic had been lost from Christmas anyway, no matter how hard we tried to capture it. This particular year someone else would be making Christmas. I would not be there for the last moment preparations, but I knew some of my older siblings would be home and would care for things.

Searching my memories, I cannot recall who took me to the airport. It may have been my oldest sister. I recall being, "dropped off." I knew if I read the signage, followed directions, and asked for help if I needed it, I would be okay. I checked in and made my way to the area where I sat and waited for my flight to be boarded. I wore a white wool A-line coat with a black furry pillbox hat and black boots and gloves. It was a time when airplanes were thought of as elite travel, not buses, so travelers wanted to look their best. I did look my best! Those were my good clothes and were not worn often. I thought I looked like Gidget and should act like her too. I put on an air of confidence, and chose to act like I know what this is all about; I fly regularly. Truth is, it was the first time I'd ever been inside an airport, and I certainly had never flown on an airplane. The only times I had ever taken flight was once on a toboggan. That was exciting. The other time was when a bunch of us were hiding in the hay mow and our oldest brother was looking for us. When we heard him enter the barn, we jumped out the haymow window. That was scary and painful. I winced at the memory. But as I sat waiting to board this plane, I acted composed. I assumed the butterflies in my stomach were only preparing me for take-off.

Once on-board, with my seatbelt secure, I said a prayer of gratitude, and asked for protection and guidance on my journey. I accepted that it was granted to me. I was never one to bother God with lots of nagging and begging. I simply asked and said thank you. It seemed to be enough. If I had God's job, I'd be annoyed by nags. I figured, neither God nor I had time for that nonsense.

I was thrilled with the speed of the plane going down the runway and with the takeoff and lift into the air. Suddenly, it didn't feel so fast anymore but we were still climbing, and everything below grew miniature. Soon we were into and surrounded by clouds. This felt even foggier than my foggiest day at home. Fortunately, it didn't last long. Next thing I knew, the sun was shining brightly on my face and nose against the window. It felt like I was in an ocean of sunlight with a fluffy blanket of cotton candy beneath me for as far as I could see. I wondered how far away heaven was from here; or, if maybe, this was it. It was beautiful! I remembered all I had seen beneath those clouds, and convinced myself it was all still there. I saw myself at the clothesline looking up at planes flying over me in a clear blue sky. Now, here I was in one of those planes. It makes you believe in possibilities.

It's only a short flight from Halifax to Boston, and it wasn't long before we were landing. There are times in life when you wish you didn't know what you know. Times when ignorance would truly be blissful. However, I knew what I knew. Landing an aircraft is considered a controlled crash. I also knew it was time to ask for a blessing for the pilot; that he would focus all his skills and training in the up-coming moments. It seemed he did just that. It was a beautiful, smooth landing; another good, first experience for me. I believe there is a reciprocal blessing that comes when we bless and have confidence in those worthy of it. In this case, the pilot did his job well and I got to live another day. It is necessary to have no doubt in ourselves or in those with whom we have consciously placed our trust. This concept is especially true in situations when we seem to have no choice or control. We always play a role in how our life unfolds through our actions, silence, stillness or blessings. It is best to be hopeful and encouraging. My fellow schoolmates taught this to me.

I followed the passengers deboarding the plane into Customs and then to the arrival area where Lily and her dad were waiting for me. Lily had our time planned, and I was happy and eager to be part of the plans. Following the half hour drive from the airport to Hopetown, I was greeted by Mariann, Lily's Mom and John, her brother After settling into their guest room, cleaning up and getting dressed to go to a high school basketball game, we relaxed and had a snack. The game was at six o'clock, and we were going for pizza with her friends following the game so we skipped supper. It was a fun evening, and that night I collapsed into bed, before eleven o'clock, totally exhausted.

The following morning I was laying awake when Lily came beating on the door to see if I was up yet. Her next plan was underway. After we ate breakfast, we walked to the end of the street to catch the bus to Farmingham. It was late morning and partly sunny but it felt cold and crispy. The snow on the sidewalks crunched and squeaked under our boots. The houses and yards along the streets were all decorated for Christmas. We hadn't waited long at the bus stop when snow flurries began falling straight down around us. There was no wind. What looked like a tour bus stopped beside us; we boarded and were seated. The bus wasn't full at this time of day, and the big, clean windows allowed me to enjoy the view. As I watched the snow fall on the Christmas streetscapes that magical feeling, I hadn't felt in years, came over me. It felt good. It was the first time, other than in fairytales, I realized that other, faraway places, also have their own special magic. It's always there, but you must be able to recognize it.

The Farmingham Shopping Mall seemed to be the last stop as everyone on the bus got off there. Lily and I did some gift shopping, and got our gift-wrapping items. The whole shopping scene felt a bit overwhelming with its vastness and availability of quality products. There were stores and brands I'd never heard of, and just so much to see. It was bustling but not crowded for the day before Christmas Eve. We caught the bus at four o'clock to return home. By then, the flurries had turned into wet, blizzardy snow. As darkness approached, the yard lights revealed their Christmas sparkle. It felt comforting. I recall thinking this is how Christmas should feel.

That evening we had dinner in the kitchen with Lily's family. Her parents and brother went out later but we didn't go because Lily had called another of our cousins who was coming by for a visit. Duke, as he was known, was older and had a car. Last summer he came to Nova Scotia with some buddies and we, Lily and I, hung out with them for a couple days. Duke arrived with one of his friends we had met last summer. We visited by the lit Christmas tree for an hour or so. I thought Duke was very handsome. Maybe it was his maturity that made him seem so attractive. He was the kind of cousin who made you want to believe Elvis, and that "kissing cousins" was alright! Every young girl has a heart throb.

On Christmas Eve afternoon we wrapped our gifts and placed them under the tree. Mariann, Lily's Mom, is Italian. Her siblings lived in the same neighborhood. In fact, her sister lived down the street. At six o'clock we all walked to her home where all of her Italian family were gathering for Christmas Eve. It wasn't a formal dinner but there were platters of food everywhere and more than enough for everyone. It was a congenial, welcoming atmosphere. It felt like Christmas Day at home. Later that evening while walking home, I felt a wave of loneliness come over me. I wondered if my family was preparing to go to midnight Mass or if they would be going in the morning. This was the first time I could remember not going to Mass at Christmas. I knew some of these people were Catholic; I knew Mariann was; yet there was no mention of going to Church. It felt like something was missing. I tried to reconcile the kindness, generosity and loving atmosphere I was experiencing with the void I was feeling: the celebration of Christmas without the celebration of Mass. Another new experience for me.

In the morning we had toast and juice in our pajamas and gathered under the tree to open gifts. Mariann had prepared the turkey and all the trimmings for lunchtime, although she allowed me to peel some vegetables to help her. We had to have our luggage packed to leave for the airport by five o'clock as our flight to Miami Beach was scheduled for seven. My second flight was fast approaching, but I already felt seasoned. It was a relaxing, uneventful flight; too dark to see anything so we read and rested. Arriving in Miami was stunning. It was ten o'clock and 72 degrees Fahrenheit, and the night was lit up as if it was broad daylight. I stood still outside the revolving airport door to briefly look around and take it all in. Momentarily, Will's brother, Harry pulled up alongside us in Will's hardtop convertible Cadillac. Harry and his wife, along with Aunt Victoria were already at the Miami Beach residence. Our luggage was put in the trunk and all five of us piled into the car with Harry. There was room to spare. When five of us had piled into the cab of Dad's truck, there wasn't room to spare.

Aunt Victoria was a quiet and wise woman. I could tell by her greeting and the smile on her face, she was happy to see me there. I thought I'd be sharing a room with Lily, but even here, I had my own room. The caretakers of the main house, who greeted us with Merry Christmas upon our arrival, had a tree and the house decorated for the season. It looked as Christmassy as I imagined Florida could look.

The caretakers left the following day and I didn't see them again until the day of our departure.

Will was a self-made millionaire who had opened his own machine shop in Hopetown. One day when he and I were sitting outside talking, and enjoying the view of the Inner Coastal Waterways, he began to reminisce. He told me how he got a bicycle when he was a young boy about twelve. He decided to get himself a paper route. He explained that he delivered papers well into his late teens through all kinds of weather. It didn't matter how bad the weather was. If there was a paper to be delivered, he delivered it. He was reliable. He said he was able to save his money; and he never looked back or had a regret. He admired hard working people because he knew the tenacity it took to keep going when things were tough. I knew he wasn't just telling me his own success story; and I appreciated his kindness. It was his way of saying why he brought me here.

Lily and I needed only to walk down the street one block and cross Collins Avenue to get to the beach, and by Boxing Day afternoon, we thought it was time to get there.

My friend from school, Angie, had lent me a new, white, two-piece bathing suit she had bought on sale at the end of the summer. It still had the tags on it. I had told her I was ready to pack my clothes for my trip but I didn't have a bathing suit to wear and didn't know where I would be able to get one. I thought I could buy one when I got to Florida. Angie told me about her new one and insisted I take it. She was sure it would fit me. The following day she brought it to school. I took it home and tried it. She was right! It went in my luggage.

Here I was now in my room in Miami Beach wearing Angie's bathing suit when I heard Lily calling my name. She was downstairs in the living room. Not being much of a screamer, I presented myself to speak to her. As I stood there in the two-piece, white bathing suit behind the glass, half-wall that overlooked the living room, I saw Lily throw her hands over her head and wave frantically to me, saying, "Go back; go back!" I had no idea what was going on, but I retreated to my bedroom. I put my cover-up and sandals on, took my packed beach bag and went downstairs. I then learned that Lily's dad and uncle were about to enter through the front living room door, and she thought I was in my underwear and wanted to save me embarrassment. Suddenly, I didn't feel so good about going to the beach wearing that swim suit. But we went; and it really didn't matter because we were the only ones there. Later I got a one-piece, blue swimsuit to save me and her any further embarrassment. We would giggle about this for decades. We beached and swam nearly every day and dined out most nights. My favorite place to eat was Joe's Stone Crab Restaurant on Washington Street in Miami Beach. It had a lively atmosphere and was fabulously delicious! I had never eaten crab before, but these buttery king crab legs were an instant hit with me. I followed this exquisite main with mile high meringue on Key Lime Pie. I felt sure I had experienced the best of life, and there really wasn't anything that could top this meal. It was seriously good!

Each morning someone came to "dust off" Will's car and make sure it looked polished. On Wednesday morning Will put the top down on the Cadillac. He, Mariann, John, Lily and I drove to Boca Raton. It was a posh resort on the beach. We spent two nights there and on the second night, dined at a supper club, with showgirls dancing.

My memories of Boca Raton are of cream and pastel pink stucco buildings stretched along a beachfront with palm trees out front, and a sandy walk from the beach. After supper on the night we arrived, Lily and I went for a walk up the beach. There were hotel bars stretched along the beachfront. I don't recall how we met them, but it seemed we were suddenly talking to a couple of guys who wanted to walk along with us. Actually, they walked us back to where we were staying; with a bit of lingering and sitting under some palm trees along the way. The guy accompanying Lily looked like a "sleaze" to me. My companion, Patrick, was very sweet. He was a handsome blend of Irish and Latin-American. He, too, came from a large family, but he was the oldest of his family. They were both spoiled, rich boys. As we were parting that evening, Lily's friend asked us to go out in his boat with them the next day. Lily was saying to me, "Do you wanna do that, blah, blah, blah…" She sounded excited. I don't know what all she said because I was focused on him. I looked into his eyes and saw all I needed to know.

I suggested, "Maybe we should first check with your parents as we don't know what they may have planned for tomorrow." She thought that made sense, but he flashed me the most hateful look I'd ever seen; confirming my suspicions. In my mind's eye, I saw sharks both inside and outside that boat, and I didn't want to be eaten by any of them.

His good-night remark was, "We'll be leaving the dock at noon. If you're not there, we won't be waiting for you."

I thought to myself: What an asshole! He already saw from the look on my face that I wouldn't be there. When we got back into the rental house, Lily immediately asked her dad if we could go boating tomorrow with these two guys we just met. Will lost it! I felt such relief. He earned my kudos for being a good parent. My Plan B, which was just formulated on the walk into the house, would not need to be utilized. It was to pretend I was throwing up in the toilet all morning.

The next day was windy and cool with sand blowing around us. We didn't go to the beach, but we did go for dinner that evening. A waitress came to take our drink orders. She asked me what I'd like from the bar. She did not ask Lily. When she walked away from our table, Lily threw her hands up. In an explosive demonstration she expressed to her parents that she was six months older than me and she had not been offered something from the bar. We all laughed but Lily did not find it funny. Will explained to her, "She just looks older than you Lil!" The legal drinking age was twenty-one. When you're fourteen that can feel like a compliment.

We had the top up on the overcast drive back to Miami Beach the next day. It was good to get back. We had a family barbeque with everyone present that night.

The following evening, we were going to a private club for dinner and would be meeting friends of Will and Mariann's, the Mahoneys. Because Will spoke about this place several times during the day, I inferred this was a rather special place, and I would be meeting good friends of theirs. I would make sure I looked my best and was not too casual. I wore a pretty dress and some gold costume jewelry. On the drive there, I sat in the back seat, directly behind Will who was driving. He addressed me to tell me more about where we were going. I leaned forward to hear him. He said, "This Club only opened a year ago, and it is a Gentile Club." A silence. "There are no Jews allowed in there," he added. I felt my body brace at that remark. I wondered what this was about. Why was he telling me this? Will was not a man I would ever expect or even consider to be a bigot or a racist. He continued to explain how only Gentile people could be members of this Club, and how long it's planning and gestation had been. He was very proud to be a part of it.

When we arrived, we waited in the foyer of the building for his other guests, the Mahoney's, to arrive. I was introduced to them upon their arrival and we were seated at our table. After taking drink orders, our server announced that the special of the evening was a pork roast dinner with all the accompaniments. Mr. Mahoney, who was seated across from me, made a face and asked, "Do you have anything else to offer? I really can't eat pork." It was said loud enough for all to hear. I saw eyes drop. But mine flashed from Mr. Mahoney to Will who was seated at the head of the table and could see everyone. Will's eyes expressed surprise and there soon rose a blush of anger onto his face. Mr. Mahoney made no eye contact with Will, but asked the server to bring him a menu. It seemed everyone else was already planning on the pork roast dinner. When I allowed my eyes to glance his way, I saw the stare of fury coming from Will's eyes. Others around the table began making small talk with each other. It seemed to me that Mr. Mahoney, working at maintaining a poker face, was insinuating he was a Jew, invited to dine at the Gentile Club where no Jews were allowed. For a fleeting second, I was humored by this brazen and rather caustic innuendo. Immediately, I realized Will was angered. This could put him in the precarious position of explaining himself to the Club Members. I didn't know the strictness of the club rules, but I sensed Will may have had concerns of his membership being revoked. I noticed he later spoke quietly to the server who seemed undisturbed by any of it. Later that night, alone with my thoughts I wondered what had happened, and what it was all about.

I had noticed earlier in the week, while shopping, or more accurately, *sightseeing,* at the nearby Bal Harbor shops, this area and Collins Avenue seemed noticeably Jewish and affluent. I wondered if Will had been refused entry to a Jewish Club or Restaurant at some point. He may have been a person who believed "money talks," and discovered, perhaps to his embarrassment, that in Miami Beach his money didn't speak Yiddish. There was no doubt he was proud to be a member of the Gentile Club. I wondered if his friend, Mr. Mahoney, as irreverent as he was, wanted to make light of a situation he believed Will took too seriously. I was left wondering if Will harbored a vendetta. Beyond curiosity, it felt like none of my business.

The next day was New Year's Eve, and we would leave late afternoon on New Year's Day to return to Boston. I was very pleased to be able to spend part of the first day of the new year in the Atlantic waters I love; and in Miami Beach, those waters are warm. Again, our return flight was at night, and it was snowy and cold in Boston. It seemed familiar but not thrilling. This Northern girl had been spoiled!

I had a couple of days before I'd be flying home to Halifax. I was able to spend an afternoon in Milford with another of my dad's sisters, Aunt Livie and my Uncle Fred. I called them that morning and they wanted me to come by to see them. Uncle Fred said they only had leftovers, but they'd like me to stay and have supper with them. It was a delicious, old-fashioned leftover supper. In fact, Uncle Fred whispered loudly to me, "I bet this is the best meal you had the whole time you were away from home."

I smiled and said, "It's really good!" I didn't mention Joe's Stone Crab to him. It was a very casual, homey and wonderful visit. It was also the last time I saw them. But for a little while after that, Aunt Livie used to write letters to me before she passed away.

On January 4th there was a snow storm, and the flight into Halifax was delayed. We eventually flew, but we couldn't land. I had to rethink my "seasoning." Apparently, life wanted to show me that there were a few spices to flying that I hadn't tried. It was a rough flight and my ears plugged up on our descent. We circled a number of times over the Halifax Harbor and near the MacDonald Bridge. We banked sharply and could clearly see the blizzard conditions out the windows. I hoped we didn't run out of fuel before we got to land. I really didn't want to be in that cold Harbor on a night like that. The thought of dying never occurred to me. But when we got clearance to land after the runway had been de-iced enough, I got nervous. The pilot knew his stuff and with a blessing or two cast his way we landed safely. I didn't know if there was going to be anyone at the airport waiting for me. It seemed that the road conditions would not be good. To my relief, my sister and her husband met me and

I drove with them to their city apartment on Connaught Avenue and spent the night there. The next day I went home. I can't tell you how or with whom because I can't remember.

You might think that was the end of my excitement, but the best was yet to come! When I arrived home that Thursday afternoon, to my shock, the natural Christmas tree was still up. It looked beautiful! My sister, Brenna was the only one home when I got there. She had everything tidy and lovely. Someone had even hung a stocking for me that remained full and untouched. Under the tree were beautifully wrapped gifts; all for me. Brenna sat with me while I opened them. But she had me open my stocking first as that was the order of things. I don't remember ever feeling so special at home. You see, at our house, a Christmas tree was NEVER allowed to be left up past midnight on New Year's Eve. It was considered "bad luck." Our mother would never hear of it. Perhaps she was just one smart woman who knew if that tree wasn't down before everyone dispersed, she'd be left with another job to do. Someone was willing to challenge the Fates to give me my Christmas at home, and it didn't go unnoticed by me.

There was never much fuss made over anything in our family. Enough time seemed to be given to all events whether it was something dreadful that happened or something most others would celebrate. There seemed to be no time for long melancholy or excessive jubilation. We could grieve or enjoy what the moment brought. But a new day was coming and we had to be there when it arrived. Many private emotions were kept to ourselves. As for my returning home from my big adventure, there was no sitting and sharing it all in detail with my siblings. They had wished me a fun time, and upon my return, asked me if I had a good trip. That was all they needed to know.

I was happy to wake up the next morning in my own room and in my own bed. It seems to me that each new sunrise is the reward for living the day before. Each day we are given a new opportunity to live, and bring the best we can of ourselves to the day. That's all that's required of us. What a blessing!

Keep Your Eyes Peeled

We were setting out on a trip Herb had dreamed of taking nearly all his life. This would be our first really long trip since he bought his Honda Gold Wing motorcycle a year ago. Besides, this occasion called for a big adventure. Our first grandchild had been born three weeks earlier, and now we were ready to drive across the country, from Halifax, Nova Scotia to Abbotsford, British Columbia to see him and welcome him into our family. I will share with you some of the amazing experiences of this epic adventure.

Aside from a downpour of rain at the end of our first day and into the next morning, we drove in the comfort of dry mid-August weather. All our garments were rolled tightly and every compartment was snugly packed. There were other things I wanted to take but Herb said we couldn't fit a cigarette paper inside that bike. I solved the problem by carrying a large leather satchel on my lap. Just like on the airlines, I called it my handbag. On our second night we took our lodging at a little Bed and Breakfast. Herb was uncomfortable with where we had to park the bike so he wanted to take all our belongings inside with us. Our gracious host offered to help carry our luggage inside. As we unpacked that bike, his eyes attested to the fact that this was the best magic he had ever seen!

We drove to Ottawa the next day and had lunch with friends. We enjoyed our reunion, but we were late getting back on the road that afternoon. Not feeling hungry at suppertime, we continued driving until nine o'clock. Just outside Sudbury we stopped at a motel. The young woman who checked us in said their restaurant closed at nine o'clock. We were tired and didn't want to backtrack into town for food. Herb asked if there was a vending machine where we could get a snack. There wasn't. We went to our room and about fifteen minutes later the same woman knocked at our door. She was carrying chicken sandwiches and a bag with cookies, milk and tea bags. The young man with her held two cups of hot water. She explained they had "found" a couple chicken sandwiches in the fridge and a few cookies in the kitchen to give us a bite to eat. Those sandwiches were fresh! Not only was this satisfying and delicious, it was complimentary. This was a sampling of the kindness and consideration we encountered as we crossed this country. The good, human decency the world knows as Canadian.

The drive from Ottawa to Manitoba took us around the North Shore of Lake Superior. The vastness of this lake is best understood by the Ojibwe name of gichi-gami for it does seem like a great sea. This entire region is vast. Yet, driving this portion of the Trans-Canada Highway we saw only three vehicles, and one was a camper; one black bear crossing the road in front of us and seemed to be aware this was turf you should run on; and finally, to my delight, there was a man selling both quart and five-pound boxes of blueberries from the tailgate of his truck parked at a clearing on the side of the highway.

Driving a motorcycle is a lot like steering life itself; you need to be aware of the big picture and what's around you, but you must keep your sights on where you intend to go. Because where you put your focus is where you will go. A passenger, however, is free to observe more detail; take notice of things a driver might miss. I spotted the "Blueberries for Sale" sign as we drove by at a pretty good clip. I said to Herb, "That guy has blueberries. Let's go back and get some!"

Herb, knowing the bike was full to capacity, asked, "Where are you gonna put blueberries?"

I replied, "In my stomach. I'm going to eat them!"

He turned the bike around. We got off for a little stretch, and made our purchase: a five-pound box! Herb insisted I shouldn't but I knew the box would sit on top of my satchel, and I could lift my helmet shield and pop berries into my mouth while he drove. We'd been married thirty-three years; he knew there was no point in making a fuss. He enjoyed some of the berries whenever we stopped. And that night we made it to our hotel in the nick of time. Blueberries don't travel really well on a motorcycle. We didn't water them, and they grew more and more dehydrated each day.

On the sixth day, we drove from Winnipeg, Manitoba and into the Province of Saskatchewan. This was the part of our journey we both anticipated might be rather boring. Live and learn!

The last fill up I could recall was in Brandon, Manitoba and now we were driving through that land where you really can watch your dog run away for three days. I don't know why anyone would want to do that, but it seemed like the right location.

Our headphones were wired into our helmets, and we always kept them on to listen to music or to talk to each other, although we could drive many miles in silence. Just when I was beginning to experience a little boredom from driving through a flat unchanging landscape, I heard Herb say, "We're low on gas. Keep your eyes peeled for a gas sign."

I said, "We have a reserve tank, don't we?"

He answered, "We're on it!"

I replied, "I'll watch; and I'll pray!"

Herb had slowed down some; I suppose in an effort to conserve what gas we had left. It was another ten minutes of driving before I spotted a sign on a little hill, to my right and far into the distance. I could barely read it, but I thought I saw the letters "GAS 4Km." I told him.

I heard the concern in his voice when Herb answered, "I hope we can make it."

I decided to keep my mouth shut about the possibility that it might have been a mirage.

We drove a few more kilometers when we saw a crossroad on the divided highway. There were some sections that were controlled access, and this was one of them. There was a dirt road that came through a field on one side and continued on to the other side of this double-laned, divided highway. There were two stop signs; one at the end of the field and the other was on the road between the divide. It also had a flashing amber light. There was another roadside sign. It said: "DOUGLAS" with an arrow pointing to the left. Herb signaled. We turned left and waited for the one lone car, we'd seen that day, go by us heading East. We crossed the highway, and the secondary road we turned on to had a sign saying "Douglas." Surprisingly, there were many twists and turns on this road. I could only imagine they were designed intentionally to add excitement. We had no clue how far it was to Douglas. After several minutes of slow driving, Herb said, "I hope this wasn't a mistake."

I asked, "What possessed you to turn onto this road?"

He answered, "The name. I think it's a good omen. I think Dad's watching over us!"

I didn't bother to offer that the name was probably linked to Tommy Douglas, an important Saskatchewanian and Canadian. I could only think there must be some irony in this: driving past August prairie fields and grasping for straws.

Some relief came when after a few more minutes we noticed buildings and a town ahead of us. The first familiar and welcoming image I saw was a Canada Post sign on the side of a building to our right. I told Herb, and we turned right, driving down below road level, on to a dirt parking area in front of the building. I glanced around and thought I wouldn't want to be here after a heavy rain. The bike was not yet parked when an angry, junkyard dog came barreling toward us. The heavy chain that had him bound fetched up about two feet from the bike giving us both a start. He was a beautiful, muscular German Shepherd that seemed trained to be vicious. Herb told him to shut up and stop barking. He didn't listen. Herb said he would stay with the bike and told me to go inside and find out where the gas station was. I listened.

I entered the building which was a small, dark room where cigarettes and candy bars were on shelves for sale. Behind a narrow counter, at the left end of this room, it appeared as if one could have their basic postal needs met. Obviously, I looked strange to the young woman standing there, even though I had removed my helmet so I wouldn't look too much like a Martian to the unsuspecting.

I said, "Hello. Could you tell me where the gas station is in town?" She stared at me and shook her head, No.

I tried again, "Do you know where the nearest gas station is?"

This time it was audible, "No."

I thought the fumes that brought me here got me farther than this is getting me. I said, "Okay. Thanks." I left.

As I stepped outside into the brightness of daylight, I saw Herb walking toward a dusty, half ton truck that just pulled in. I watched as a young guy jumped out of the truck.

Herb greeted him and asked, "Is there a gas station here in town?"

The guy replied, "No; but we're building one: just down the street."

Herb said, "I can't wait. I came into town on fumes. I've got to get some gas somewhere."

Just as you would picture it, they both leaned on the cargo bed of that truck and pondered how this problem could be solved. I'm not quite sure how it happened; if Herb had noticed the five-gallon containers in the back of the truck, or if the driver just remembered he had them there, but the next thing I heard was Herb offering to buy some gas from him. I waited with gratitude while Herb poured some of the strangers' gas into the bike tank, gave him five dollars and a handshake. The only thing Herb said to me on the drive back out of Douglas was, "I knew it was a good omen!"

It was about five o'clock when we got back on the Trans-Canada. We drove about another half hour when we were able to fill up at a gas station.

Whether it was to make up for lost time, or because he was feeling so darn lucky, or simply excited about all the gas he now had in his tank, something inspired Herb to drive like a bat out of hell. This was 2004 and not all of Highway 1, the Trans-Canada through Saskatchewan, was completely twinned. On a section of undivided highway, we came upon some tractor trailers merely driving the speed limit. They had themselves a convoy. There was no way we could see just how many trucks were ahead of us, but that didn't stop Herb from making the decision to pull out and pass them. I counted nine and may have missed a couple as I got distracted by the headlights coming toward us. In this landscape, my perceptions had no way of informing me what the distance between us and the oncoming vehicle might be.

The strangest thing happened. I had never before experienced such quiet stillness within me. I remember thinking two things: This is where we might die; and Herb knows what he has to do. Yet, I was as calm as an early morning harbor between the change of tides. There wasn't a ripple in me. If those truck drivers had glanced our way, they might have seen their own reflections in my stillness. The music was turned off. There could be no distractions. There was no room for error.

We were beside the cab of the front truck of the convoy when I first saw the driver of the approaching car. It was then that Herb cut in front of the truck. I looked as the car went by us. It was the RCMP. There was no roof light, only a dash light. At the speed we were doing, it all happened really fast. It was about the same speed with which the calm left me and panic struck. Suddenly, I had to tell myself to stay calm. We remained silent and thankful for a few seconds. I saw Herb check his rearview mirror. It was then I asked, "Is he turning around?"

Herb answered, "No. He's gotta get home to supper."

I grinned. Then I thought he's probably calling ahead for someone to pull us over. I asked Herb, "Do you think we could slow down now?" He thought so, and did.

That night we arrived at my sister's home in Calgary. We had a pleasant and relaxing visit with her and her family. It took only minimal persuasion for me to agree to toss out the remaining dehydrated blueberries. It was late morning when we continued on our way to Abbotsford to meet the newest addition to our family. A family that still had all its members.

There was road construction on the highway through the mountains. While we sat waiting in traffic, a black bear strolled along the edge of the highway next to the idling vehicles. I felt vulnerable as we were the only ones on a bike. I also felt pleased that I had discarded the blueberries in Calgary. It had been a little nerve-wracking driving through Roger's Pass on a motorcycle, but we were glad we did it. The rest of the drive through the Canadian Rockies was spectacular beauty.

At 8:30 p.m. on August 18th we drove into the garage of our son's home. Our grandson was one month old. We had just removed our helmets and jackets when our daughter-in-law came into the garage and placed our grandson in my arms. It was a moment of rapture. A moment of falling in love. I know of no words that can completely express what I felt, but I have a picture that says it all. My daughter-in-law also snapped a photograph of our meeting. Each time I look at it, I recapture the natural, uninhibited joy of that moment. We had only a week to spend cuddling, adoring and memorizing the sweetness of this precious miracle called Andrew. Herb got to see him sleeping in the cradle he built and shipped out to them months earlier. Andrew would be the first of our six grandchildren to be cradled in the warmth of the love of their grandad's wood-working project.

The drive home, a drive which often feels like the best part of any trip to me, was not a joyful one. I cried for three days and the skies cried with me. The weather supported my sorrow. We cheered ourselves, on the remaining days of the trip home, by looking forward to December when they would be coming to visit and spend the holidays with us.

We never spoke about the ride through Saskatchewan for the longest time. But when we were back home, I heard Herb telling someone about our trip, and that particular experience. My eyes were peeled as I heard him mention, for the first time, the speed we were traveling. I offered another prayer of thanks, and felt that being back home was a good omen.